Pornography of the Gaze

Pornography of the Gaze is an unflinching, fantastical meditation on love, sex, and death. It is composed as an explicit re-writing of *Histoire de l'Oeil,* the French surrealist classic by Georges Bataille, widely regarded an erotic masterpiece of the 20th Century. Here, the novelistic account similarly charts a wild, lewd and transgressive journey of two young lovers and their notable acquaintances. In doing so, it draws upon and implicates a series of texts, incidents and accidents: all revolving around the still unanswered question of the gaze; what it means to look and be looked at. Susan Sontag once wrote of the 'considerable gain in truth' to be made from attending to the literary genre of pornography. Nearly a hundred years on from Bataille's original story, the verve of such writing is surely never more urgent a response to contemporary utilitarian, restrictive, and homogeneous ways of living.

Pornography of the Gaze

By Lord B.

With an essay by Sunil Manghani

Pécuchet Press

Published by Pécuchet Press, England.

ISBN 978 1 7397 6690 0 (Paperback)
ISBN 978 1 7397 6691 7 (Kindle)
ISBN 978 1 7397 6692 4 (ePub)

A CIP catalogue record for this publication
is available from the British Library.

Contents

Part One   THE TEXT   5

A Cat's Tale
Beached Wardrobe
Laura's Kitchen
Orbiting the Sun
Blood Line
Time-lapse
Laura
(Open Eyes of) Vertigo
Delicacies of the Cock
Flung Ink
Rue de Richelieu
The Lesson
Legs of a Phage

Part Two   PREPARATION   103

Barthes / Bataille   123
by Sunil Manghani

1. THE TEXT

A Cat's Tale

I grew up very much in my own world (a muddle of fact and fiction), and as much as I remember I was nervous of anything sexual. Yi must have been nearly eighteen when I met her and so a couple of years older. It happened at a party in an old house somewhere in X. With furtive, downcast eyes, I sat quietly watching all the adults dancing to records, smoking and drinking.

I spied Yi a few times through the mess of people. Mostly she sat quite still, expressionless. A couple of times she realised I was looking at her; I thought perhaps she shared my anxiety at seeing her (though it was probably not the case). In the early hours I came to be sitting next to her. We were giving a lift to Yi and her mother since they lived nearby. I sat in the middle of the back seat as I was the smallest. And there I was, my legs awkwardly between the two front seats and my left thigh hard up against Yi. She seemed barely to notice me and did not utter a word throughout. I was breathing in, trying to keep from touching her. She had a plaster cast that came above the knee, which rubbed against my leg.

The bare, milky skin of her thigh above the cast flickered with the florescent hue of the street. It was a warm night. The air carried her sweet, sweaty scent. My anxiety rose as I imagined what the whole of her naked body must smell like. It struck me that I could run my hand above the cast and, by lifting slightly her pinafore, I might see what was otherwise obscured. A book I had been reading secretly at the time ran vividly through my mind: 'It was extremely hot. She put a saucer of milk on a small bench, and, with her eyes fixed on me, sat down without my being able to see her burning buttocks under the skirt, dipping into the cool milk'. I reached under Yi's skirt and briefly felt the dip between her thighs.

At that point the car stopped and Yi was helped out onto her crutches. Everyone waved and whispered goodnight as the car moved off. I shifted over to where Yi had been sitting and watched her through the window, in her short pinafore, grappling with the crutches. The wet sensation between my legs was undeniable.

The next day I went to find Yi's house. Dark rings hung around my eyes. She peered at me for a while from the doorway. Then, dropping her head to one side, I could have sworn she said: 'I don't want you to toss off without me next time'. With that she invited me in and our love life began. It was so intimate and intense we never let a week go by without seeing each other. We rarely communicated between meeting up, but we just knew, when we saw each other, that we felt the same. Mostly we went to Yi's house and took walks nearby. In the woods one day we saw a dead fox. Its head was severed from the body and one of its eyes was missing. I told Yi about my book and described the scene where the two lovers crash their car into a cyclist: 'an apparently very young and very pretty girl. Her head was almost totally ripped off by the wheels'. We stood still a long time, absorbed by the sight of the corpse. *The horror and the despair at so much bloody flesh, nauseating in part, and in part very beautiful, was fairly equivalent to our usual impression upon seeing one another.*

Yi was slender, enchanting, ambivalent. She took little interest in make-up and while she possessed all number of expensive clothes, she would sling things on in the most nonchalant manner, at times adapting a skirt as a shawl, and a shirt as a dress. While there was nothing deeply heart-breaking in her eyes or voice, on a sensual level she could turn the faintest thing into something suggestive. Possessed of a deep sexuality, she revelled in all things that came to the senses, the sight of blood, the smell of food, the sounds of the city, and the touch of skin. I saw her shudder and writhe (as I did too) that very first day she took me inside. Perhaps we only exchanged the briefest looks then, but we never calmed down from that day on. Although, I must point out, it was some time before I penetrated her. Instead, we indulged in all kinds of unusual behaviour.

One day I discovered a childhood toy of Yi's — it was a little cat. Thereafter, in those brief relaxed moments after orgasm we would spot him looking down upon us. We took it in turns to animate the little stuffed toy. He possessed a strange, rather polite voice. We'd gently pivot the back of his head as he spoke. His beady eyes would appear to wink at us; he really seemed to be alive. Sometimes we burst out laughing at the things he would make us say, but our ventriloquism also offered a degree of wisdom, which otherwise neither of us could muster.

As autumn arrived we struck up something of a ritual. We went to the shop around the corner to buy a night's supply of crisps, chocolate, and candy. Then we'd settle in to watch the television. We sat together with our horde strewn about the floor (the scent of sugar palpable). Gorging ourselves, we would wait for the daily instalment of phosphorous green pictures from somewhere in the Middle East.

There were various maps to analyse and reports from journalists in bullet-proof vests. They gave all the signs of being somewhere exotic or treacherous, as if speaking live from a sinking ship. But mostly they were hauled up in a fancy hotel. We always preferred to see the pictures from the infra-red cameras on the front of missiles. We gasped in awe as one seemed to turn a corner as it flew low in the middle of a city before the picture then went fuzzy. During these nights we'd kiss, lick and fondle each other, yet always with one eye staring intently at the screen.

Each night a fat General stood in front of a TV screen to show highlights. I always enjoyed the fact we were watching TV through a TV. Taking crisps and sweets in our hands we listened avidly to the latest stories and watched grainy film clips of bridges and buildings suddenly turn to big white streaks, as if the roll of film were igniting. One night, the General showed what looked like a toy car reaching the far side of a bridge, before the picture then flashed white and the screen went blank. 'That's the luckiest guy in the city!', he bellowed. I remember thinking here *is* god, but to whom no one could surrender. The glint of his white teeth reminded me of the spaghetti Westerns when the bad guys would fire off their guns. In the swirl of smoke, there would be wild, manic laughter; laughter that always went on much longer than necessary. Much longer than it would actually take to kill the people.

One particular night there was a huge green explosion. It lit up the whole of the living room, and on the screen was a silhouette of vehicles in convoy. As the night-vision camera came back into focus we saw the face of a melted man with no eyes; his hands on the wheel of his truck, frozen, looking out awkwardly through the blown-out windshield. This murdered face was a brittle mask that spoke to me of how war is not for land; that we can never properly kill one another.

'Of course, none of it is real', announced Yi. 'Imagine: a war when no one turns up!'.

She was sucking a single crisp as she spoke, licking off all the flavour before putting it back in her mouth. I thought how I wanted to be in her mouth. Yi was aware of my erection and looked back at me playfully. She stood up and bent herself over, stretching out towards the TV. Her buttocks pushed out towards me.

'Put your fingers inside', she said. I did so and masturbated at the same time.

'Why don't you pee over me?' she said.

'I can,' I answered, 'but with you like this, it'll get on your dress'.

'So what?' she called back.

I did as she asked, and at that very moment as I flooded over her back and down her legs, we heard the doorbell ring.

'Please don't move', Yi insisted.

We heard voices in the corridor and then as the living

room door opened a ravishing blonde girl appeared. 'Your friend, Laura, is here', came a voice from somewhere in the hallway.

Still contracted in our dreadful position, Laura – who was to become the most affecting of our friends – collapsed into the room, sobbing. Yi untangled herself from our pose and away from the TV. She rushed to embrace her friend. Transfixed, I watched as Yi ran her hands about this self-abandoned body. Laura was dressed in black trousers and a high-neck jumper.

'Please, Yi spoke softly, 'please don't cry. We can play together…'

Yi pulled Laura up from where she was slumped and brought her over to a small rug. She quietly instructed her to kneel on all fours.

'There', Yi said, 'Don't move'.

She then collected up all our confectionary and placed it neatly upon Laura's back as if she were a table at a tea party. Next, she hitched up her wet dress and pulled me towards her. Like an acrobat she bent herself over Laura, as if one table stacked upon another. The smell of sugar mixed with the smell of urine and wet clothes. I was trying to get myself hard as I thrust my fingers back inside of Yi, but I was distracted by the smoothness of Laura's arse, which, despite being pushed up towards me, revealed nothing. Just the engulfing, shiny curvaceous nothingness of her skin-tight trousers, which run all the way to her upturned heels.

'I can't see what you are doing', Laura complained, still half crying.

'Take the magazine', Yi suggested.

In that dark room, bent over the table-like form of Laura, with only the light of the television to see by, Yi and I entered a brutal frenzy of pleasuring ourselves. The pixels on the large TV glared back at us, bathing us in an unhealthy green glow. Still mesmerized by the sublimity of Laura's arse, I found it hard to come. But when I finally stood back it had covered us all. Yi, still bent over, watched as a single, thick globule fall from between her legs. It landed with a satisfying sound beside the rug upon the polished floor. In a nasally, but excited tone, she offered a little cheer.

'In the country of the blind, the one-eyed man is king!', she sang.

Beached Wardrobe

It was during this time that we became enamoured with a rather quaint parlour. We gorged ourselves there on stacks of pancakes lathered in cream and berry fruits, the juices of which would stain our hands and mouths and would inevitably end up on our genitals. Yi would frequently stand at the counter to watch the pancakes being made, chatting causally with the staff and always swooning audibly as the eggs were broken and beaten in a large bowl. On one occasion, while no one was looking, she leant across and stole an egg, and then, bending towards me, placed it between the crack of her buttocks. While she amused herself with this trick, I rubbed my cock directly before her face and the moment my come splattered her face she came too, and the egg smacked to the floor.

One of the older women working in the parlour caught us in this act a few times, but never uttered a word. Perhaps she never got passed the shock of it, or perhaps she was just too worldly-wise to care. When we tried to clean up our mess, she would usher us away and quietly attend to the spilt egg. On one particular day, as Yi stared with greater attention than before to the whisking of the eggs, she peed straight onto the floor. As the puddle of urine spread about her shoes and having soaked her socks and the bottom of the counter, the same old woman looked at us with such dismal eyes. Yet her desperate expression only egged us on, which is to say, Yi burst out laughing and I could not stop myself from running my fingers around her thighs and inside her to feel all the remaining wetness.

It had been a whole week without us seeing Laura when we bumped into her on the street. The blonde girl, seemingly timid on the outside, held such a pensive stare. Yi immediately embraced her with unusual warmth.

'Laura, please don't be mad,' she whispered. 'What happened the other day was absurd. Please let us be friends. I will never lay a finger on you again.'

Laura gave no immediate reply and it was difficult to read the look she continued to give us, except to say it enthralled us. Catching each other's eye, we knew instinctively, Yi and I, *nothing would make us shrink from achieving our ends.*

In those days we held numerous tea parties, although of course we never actually drank tea. Various good-looking boys and girls around our age would turn up, and Yi would ply them with vodka, wine and champagne; whatever could be found in her mother's store. These parties were never held without our friend Laura joining, though she would always move quietly in and about the spaces between us all, and always, to the best of my knowledge, remained sober. Yi would play loud music and dance about half-naked. The other girls followed her lead and while I could not see through their underwear at their age it bound to them laxly without hiding much. Only Laura refused to dance, but then, in amongst the revelry this would go unnoticed. Yi would get ever drunker and pose all sorts of dares.

'I bet I can pee into my hands and pour enough into this champagne glass', she would announce. To which one of the boys would invariably challenge her. Most times Yi would win and always the penalty for losing involved her pulling their trousers down.

'Why do you look at m/e?' She would demand in-between faint hiccups, 'your hands touch m/y clitoris, m/y labia. Round your shaft you think you wrap m/y duodenum. And if *I* pant you think *I* am yours!'.

Despite the ridiculousness and innocence of such scenes, it usually prompted Laura to beg to leave and on one occasion a more dramatic stand-off ensued.

'We won't touch you Laura,' Yi said, 'I promised you that. Why do you want to leave?'

But the silence of Laura obliterated anything further that could be said out loud. At which point Yi whispered something to Laura, who then slipped across the room to a large antique bridal wardrobe where she shut herself in. Through the keyhole could be seen one bright blue eye looking back at us all. This became her vantage point when things got too much.

I should say, despite any apparent clarity with which I might have described things, we were always very drunk and too preoccupied to really notice what was going on. By this point, naked boys and girls would be sucking and licking one another, a singular body of glands, ganglia, and lobes, and secretions of mucosae, spittle, snot, lymph, milk and pleura. Yi would either collapse into a corner in a daze or be seen dancing drunkenly with her fingers inside herself. In the early hours, after all the debauchery of tumbling bodies, lofty legs and arses, wet skirts and come, Yi and I would unlock the wardrobe to find Laura, usually naked, smelling of piss and come, with lines of mascara dribbled about her swollen eyes. On one such occasion, indeed the penultimate time, she was perched in the wardrobe fully clothed; a little unkempt, but quite still. Upon seeing us, she displayed a sickly sense of terror and let out the most inhuman shriek.

Yi and I spoke little of the matter in the coming days, yet nonetheless agreed we had to do something about the wardrobe, the inhumanity of which, as it stood soundless and heavy in the room, grew more and more.

Yi's first thought was to fill it with concrete, to make a perfect version of the inside of itself, but we talked of the inevitable practicalities, of the sheer hard work. Yi lost her enthusiasm. Instead, she reached for the telephone.

'Operator! Operator! I want a removal company...'

While I hardly knew what she was planning I sat before Yi smiling, looking forward to whatever she had in mind for the great bulk of the thing.

'Hello? Can you come right away? I want to move my wardrobe. It is an antique.'

She repeated her request several times, just to make sure, and assured them it would be worth their while. Afterwards we lazed about for several hours and Yi tried on numerous outfits, though none were quite right she said.

As the day was beginning to fade three muscular men arrived in their truck. We showed them in, and it took all three of them to heave the wardrobe out. With great effort they hauled it up onto the back of their truck, with it standing upright, and tethered it with lots of ropes like a scene from Gulliver's Travels. They then drove off, heading directly into the setting sun. At which point, Yi emerged from the neighbour's garden wheeling a moped and beckoned for me to get on. She kick-started the thing first time and we rode as fast as we could to catch up with the wardrobe, which was still just in sight, silhouetted against the big orange ball of the sinking sun.

When we arrived at the beach, directly below the cliff, the sun was just dipping into its horizon and causing ripples of itself across the rolling waves. I looked up at the deepening blue dome of the sky that held everything inside. I remember feeling as if I were inside a midsummer version of a snow globe. I wondered what lay beyond this vast aperture of our lives.

We ditched the moped in the sand, and perhaps inspired by the bloody sun, we both thought we might set fire to it, only we were too distracted. Peering up at the cliff we watched as the removal truck parked up. The three men staggered with the load, before leaving the wardrobe defiantly upon the very edge of the cliff and duly drove away. Yi sighed happily and then taking a deep breath as if she were to begin a sermon, she stopped short:

'Look!" She cried, pointing starkly with an outstretched finger. It was hard to discern at first due to the rippling light of the sun, but something was not quite right.

'It's moving! It's rocking!' Yi exclaimed.

We raced as fast as we could to the top of the cliff. As we neared the wardrobe, gasping, holding our aching sides, we recovered enough to rip open the doors. Sure enough, inside was Laura. She looked quite white and stared out at us, bewildered by the daylight. In having flung the doors open so violently we had caused the wardrobe to pivot all too dangerously. We each grabbed an arm and pulled Laura towards us, except, to our eyes, as the massive deadly box fell over the side of the cliff and plummeted below, it seemed as if Laura had stopped still in mid-air, the whole moment a freeze-frame. Then came the dramatic pound of the wardrobe hitting the ground.

Despite its descent the antique wardrobe, strong as it was, lay deep in the sand, largely in-tact. The two doors were gaping open, strained upon their hinges. The mirror, fixed to the back of one of these doors, had cracked cleanly into a series of zigzags. Looking over the top of the carcass of the wardrobe we saw multiple versions of ourselves fan across the broken shards.

With the sun now setting ever lower, still clinging to the last of its flame, we instinctively removed our clothes and clambered into the wardrobe. The lapping of the incoming tide made it both boat and bath. Laura was trembling and shivering feverishly. Upon her face was again the residue of that sickly horror we'd seen before. I pulled her towards me to keep her warm and asked her what she had being doing in the wardrobe. She was all but speechless, mumbling only to herself something about her words being all dead. Yi stretched out opposite me, her delicate feet wrapped around my cock, toying with it idly. In her hand she held a shard of mirror. She played with her hair, trying different lengths and poses. All the while she sang made-up sea shanties. In this way we swam in the bottom of the wardrobe, in the same shallow waters.

Yi went on with her songs even after she could no longer see her reflection in the now failing light. My hands were lost before my eyes, yet still I could sense Yi's smile as she sang her silly songs. *Now the sun had sunk, I recall: Sky and sea were indistinguishable. The waves breaking spread their white fans far out over the shore, sending white shadows into the recesses of sonorous caves and then rolled back sighing over the shingle. At the cliff's edge there was an equal murmur of air, of water that had been cooled in a thousand glassy hollows of mid-ocean. As if there were waves of darkness in the air, darkness moved on, covering houses, hills, trees, as waves of water wash round the sides of some sunken ship. Them, too, darkness covered.*

Laura's Kitchen

Each week I travelled across town to the art school, spending two full days painting from the model. The smell of oils as you reached the studio soon became quite reassuring. The class was held in the annex of W. School of Art, a building dating to the 1930s. It stood on the corner of a road facing opposite to a community hall, where, by chance, an amateur dramatic society put on badly acted plays.

We had to take frequent breaks to give the model time to stretch and have a cigarette. Each time she would go behind a barricade of misshapen easels and then reappear in a silky dressing grown. I never understood why she would go away to change to and from her clothes. I only knew how Yi took her clothes off at any time. Once the model was settled (with arbitrary objects placed around her) we worked for what seemed like hours. Despite the opportunity to just stare, we spent most of the time looking inwardly, painting earnestly, high on turps, listening to music on headphones that leaked a litany of tinny pop and hip hop. I'd often hear some of the other boys in the class talk crudely about the girls we knew (or about movie stars). But they never spoke of the models before us.

In between a line of battered easels, with the sun coming sharply through the large windows, the art teacher sat quietly at a table, like a cubist painting, reading his newspaper and eating an orange (the one accent of colour in the room). From time to time the model would whisper that she needed a break. The teacher would get up apologetically and affect an air of authority. Occasionally, he wandered around, going from easel to easel. He was not a very attractive man. His breathing was laboured and his eyes lacked colour. He had no qualms in taking your brush and making direct changes. Cooped up as we were, one easel to the next, it was difficult to get the foreshortening right. On numerous occasions, he would take the palette knife and simply scrap a portion of paint away, or even, in some cases, the whole of the picture. The other classmates would shuffle in their seats, sharing in the humiliation. 'At your level', he would proclaim, 'you can't worry about starting again'. And he'd tirelessly remind us of notable artists who even to this day did the same. As time went by, I started to enjoy the act of removing the paint. I liked how there always remained a stain of what was painted before, and I always preferred the process of just beginning to mark out a pose, making those first intuitive lines. The long, drawn-out process of working up a painting bored me, and subsequently I rarely finished anything, while my classmates went on to produce little masterpieces.

In truth, I never felt so calm than during these days. Yet, I never worked out where the model was looking; where *her* gaze fell. It appeared never to land anywhere in the room, which became an infinite fascination. There was a parade of different models each week (all women, except one man who oddly sat in his underwear). But it was Laura who I always hoped to see. The first time she walked through the door we both stopped still (all the things we'd done with Yi racing through our minds). But she smiled and went to change. Her lithe body and delicate muscular forms (especially her arms) made it that much easier to draw an outline. I hear artists have their signature marks; gestures that do not lie. Mine is the line from the round of the neck to the arm. It always feels – literally feels – such an intuitive line to follow, and Laura's was the most beautiful of all.

In the afternoons we took a long break to head over to the nearby café. One day, quite out of the blue, one of our classmates, whose name I never did know, said he could take us somewhere better and that we could go in his car. He was tall and rather good looking. He made the rest of us look shabby. The idea that one of us was old enough to drive, let alone own a car, was exhilarating. A friend and I followed out from the café to the car. It was a gleaming red BMW. The sort of thing I'd only seen in movies.

Looking back, I realise it was folly to drive any distance during our limited afternoon break. And, then it happened. Without time to think, the humdrum side streets became the site of agony. Without any outward sign of bravado, our driver stepped hard on the accelerator. He sped through the grid of narrow residential roads. As we headed to a cross-road he never slowed, never intended to. If anything, he sped up. A car perpendicular to us slammed hard into ours. There was not a great deal of visible damage to our car, instead, tank-like, we had smashed to pieces the bonnet of the other.

A man languished strangely at the wheel. It seemed odd he didn't get out.

Of course, I saw none of this at first. My friend was in the front passenger seat. As I looked up at him, he was holding his chest and wincing. The force of the whiplash had rendered him speechless. At the wheel, our driver had a bloody nose, while I had been hurled from the back of the car, ending up like a disjointed toy in the well of my friend's seat. Upside down, I opened the passenger door and spidered out. It was then, on the side of the road, that we looked at the scene. Apart from asking each other blankly if we were okay, we had nothing to say. I vaguely recall giving a brief statement to a policeman. The flashing blue lights made me queasy.

Dazed and aching, I limped back to the school. I never spoke of the incident from that day on (even when I received the invitation in a little brown envelope to attend court). As I reached the entrance, I saw Laura. She was just putting out a cigarette.

'What happened?' she asked.

I muttered something to suggest it was nothing.

'Wait here', she said, and disappeared into the building, only to re-appear wrapped in a coat and with a bag across her shoulder.

'Come on,' she said, taking my hand, guiding me back through the same criss-crossing roads I'd emerged from.

It was on reaching Laura's apartment that I began to feel the pain I was in. My head was throbbing. I felt a little sick and my hair was caked in dried blood. Laura brought me into the kitchen and said she'd get me some tea and a painkiller.

'I was told you don't like boys', I blurted out.

Laura returned an incredulous look: 'Take these and sit down'.

Before I knew it, she dragged me into a chair positioned in front of the kitchen counter.

'Do I have to tie you up, or do you promise not to move?'

She was quite matter of a fact and was already rolling up her sleeves and putting on an apron. She stirred several teaspoons of sugar into the tea, telling me it was for the shock.

'Don't move. Not a muscle! Keep your head very still, like a movie camera, keep your eyes on me'.

She then went to the other side of the counter. She stood motionless, taking a few slow breaths like a gymnast before they take a run-up. She then proceeded to demonstrate the use of the various kitchen utensils with strange, forceful gestures. Her eyes glazed over, and her voice modulated flatly. Having sat through this charade for some time, not knowing if it was meant to arouse, unnerve, or even soothe me, I began to see her more as a set of lines and shapes. She yanked a ladle for a second time, gesturing as if scooping the skin off an imaginary boiling pot, flicking the contents behind her in a strangely calm violence. I couldn't help but see a resemblance to the King of Pop. Their lithe forms both seemed to possess a peculiar and fluid human nature; each presenting their own definite, obsessive, and *apparently* repeatable lexicon, yet that none could decipher, nor replicate.

Aching, slumped on the kitchen counter, I woke from what felt like a long sleep. By this time Yi had arrived to see how I was after the accident. But she was distracted by Laura who held a little movie camera – an 8mm camera, as she told us. Yi danced around the room wanting both to take hold of it and yet equally to be watched by the bedevilling little device. Like a bulky gun, Laura pointed it at us and pressed the trigger. She peered through the viewfinder while the shiny, convex lens stared at us, tracked us, with its swollen eye. Yi, clapping her hands, swooned at the click-clacking sound as the film rolled. I read somewhere if you opened it up 'a stream of film would pour from the back of the box and dissolve slowly (like the memory of a dream)'.

'Film us, film us' Yi urged as she turned to me with a huge grin.

She was pulling at my trousers and getting on her knees. Yi gave strict instructions to Laura:

'Don't move, keep it looking at us', she commanded, 'film him in slow motion getting hard. Don't stop'.

But as she thrust her mouth over me, as I felt her teeth and saliva, I became aware Laura was filming directly into my face. I was looking both pleasured and pained at the same time. I didn't want Yi to stop, but like Yi, I wanted the camera to look at what she could see. I beckoned to Laura to move, but she just stared ever harder through that one eye: her looking at me, while I looked at her filming. When I could hold it no longer, I pushed Yi onto the floor and pulled her tight skirt up over her thighs.

'Film this Laura, film me!' Yi called out.

Thrusting my tongue inside of Yi, I kept looking back over my shoulder. Laura held the camera in the same fixed position looking out to where I had previously been standing. As the film whirred and clicked through the mechanism it was looking at nothing. Then, Laura slowly started to move the camera. She didn't turn it upon the scene we were making. Instead, she stretched out her arm as far as she could and turned the lens back upon herself. She filmed herself looking at us as we came.

We must have drifted to sleep while still holding each

other. Our hands, curled about one another's genitals, were all covered in come. We awoke to find the apartment empty. Yi gave me a kick.

'Look,' she said, 'something is wrong!'.

Laura had gone. Her coat and bag were no longer there. The kitchen was bare. We knew immediately something had happened. Later, we were told the circumstances of Laura's incarceration and even the name of the institution. But from that very first day we thought about Laura: her obsessiveness, the loneliness of her gaze, the possibilities of getting her, helping her escape her own way of seeing, perhaps. Days later, when I tried to climb upon Yi in her bed, she deftly slipped from beneath my grasp:

'You think I am your object, little man?' she cried, 'I'm not doing that here, *in a bed like this, like a housewife and mother!* This parade of yours has nothing to do with me, everything to do with you. I'll only do it with Laura!'

'What do you mean? I asked.

I was a little hurt, not because she turned me away, but because I actually agreed with her. Yi now returned to me. She splayed herself across my body, and looking down at me affectionately said in a soft, dreamy voice:

'Listen, she won't be able to help staring when she sees us... doing it. Laura would say herself: *the time has come for us to take over the show and exhibit our own fears and desires'*.

Laughing happily, and staring down on me, I felt Yi's hot liquid run across my legs. When she had finished, I too watered her body, which she complaisantly directed across her soft skin. Covered in our fluids in this way, she touched herself in a cathartic frenzy.

'You smell like Laura's Kitchen', Yi cheered after a deep, shuddering climax, her face now sunk between my legs, her nose nestling against my wet anus.

It was then that Yi and I both knew we didn't want to have sex without Laura there to see us. And in that moment, I began to feel a heaviness I'd not felt before. As I withdrew and saw my come dribble from within, I felt myself a stranger. It had started to rain, the sound of it tapping against the window. I lay on the floor next to Yi. We listened to the rhythmic sound. I thought back to the time in the kitchen. I began to wonder where I had really been, whether I had been there with Yi, or rather in the camera, through the eyes of what Laura saw. I was physically at rest, but nothing more. Dreary, sad, yet tender, my eyes wandered over Yi's face plaintively. She looked back, her eyes betraying a sight of beauty.

'It is raining', I said.

Yi ran her hand over my arm. The room felt extraordinarily quiet. I could have lain there for hours, as if nothing mattered, as if my living *were smeared away into the beyond, near and quite lovable. This strange, gentle reaching-out to a little death was new to me.*

'We must go', said Yi.

I replied affirmatively but did not move. And I rehearsed long-forgotten lines: 'Life seemed a shadow, day a white shadow; night, and death, and stillness, and inaction, this seemed like *being*. To be alive, to be urgent and insistent—that was *not-to-be*. The highest of all was to melt out into the darkness and sway there, identified with the great Being'.

Orbiting the Sun

All we could think of was Laura, and our imaginations ran wild. We pictured her shooting herself, the identification in the morgue, the big spectacle of the funeral. Finally, however, we had word of her whereabouts. She was to appear at a large museum in the city. In little over an hour our train pulled into the station. The sunlight shafting through the skylights was quite dazzling. Stepping from the train I panicked momentarily as Yi was nowhere to be seen. Yet, as I spun around, with the crowds filing out from the carriages, she was standing right next to me. I was a little perturbed as to how I might have made such a mistake. How could she have been there all along, I thought, when I'd distinctly not seen her a second before. We traversed our way through the murmuration of people – like a cloud of extras from a poorly dubbed movie; everything in its place yet somehow always elsewhere too. It was a short walk before we saw the museum rise before us. It stood proudly across the glistening river, its massive complex a former power station from the middle of the twentieth century.

After having finally reached the building it took us a great deal of time to find our way in. We thought we'd found the main entrance, but it was sealed. Through the glass we faintly saw the shapes of bodies drifting about. We had circled the entire circumference, finding numerous other entrances similarly closed, when eventually we discovered an inclined ramp, which oddly we must have missed before. This unassuming threshold, like a conjuring trick, led us into the heart of the building, into its huge atrium. It was at least 30 metres high. And, albeit an industrial, drab interior, staring up at its pinnacle gave me the same dizzying sense of looking up at the wealth of a cathedral.

We passed a security guard who gave us a friendly nod, as if we knew one another. As we entered the space we were instantly bathed in a throbbing orange glow. We were each about to remark upon this fact when we spied a large banner hanging down from one of the upper gantries. It wafted lightly in the gusts of wind that came periodically from the doorway. There was no getting away from the fact we recognised the face printed upon the banner, and down the left side of which, set out like the cut-out words of a newspaper, was the strange phrase 'The Inter-disciplinary Gaze', along with the details of an event due to take place that evening.

Strewn across the floor of the atrium were hundreds of languid bodies. People of all shapes and sizes were lying quietly, some seemingly having brought their own towels or blankets. They were soaking up the rays of the cosmic orb held just beneath a vast mirror high up in the ceiling. It was this artificial sun that had given the warm glow to our faces as soon as we had walked in. We headed across to a large, yet somehow claustrophobic domed ticket office. Unlike the drenching light of the atrium, this welcome area provided a more perfunctory and muted setting. A single shaft of sunlight (real or not, it was hard to tell), glanced across a circular, perspex shielded desk. The office was deserted. Yi banged vigorously on a little silver bell. Eventually a young woman in a red blazer appeared.

'I'm so sorry to have kept you', she said, a little out of breath. '…our director would sincerely have wished to greet you herself. But what with the arrangements…'

The woman was evidently quite concerned for us, but equally as my gaze circled the booth — its full 360 degrees — I watched her turning over in her mind a particular incident. It was only a momentary episode, but one she and her husband rehearsed numerous times. Saying goodbye, she kissed the sweet-smelling forehead of their son, who was moving about energetically in the highchair. Her husband meanwhile stared straight through it all; that same look as if to say: 'are you really leaving me with all this?'. They had the same conversation about the cost of childcare, that it just did not add up, despite work having value in itself. She slipped on her coat and turning to say goodbye simply gave a silent combined look of love and apology. She left the house — as so many times before — feeling all at once elated and guilty. As she churned over this riddle, against the grain of her professionalism, I felt as if the room was spinning ever so slightly, a singular, clockwise rotation. Then abruptly all stopped: Yi informed that in fact we wished to *purchase* tickets. At which point the woman's previously apologetic tone quickly evaporated. Flustered, she told us it was quite out of the question.

We made our excuses and fled. There, huddled into my arms, it was the first time I witnessed Yi racked by anything other than her own lewdness. Our hearts were beating in confusion as we stood motionless, bathed again in the virtual light of the atrium; the face on the banner loomed over us. The fact that Laura was here, yet we were no closer to her, raged through us like a dementia that craned its colours throughout this mirthless cathedral of art. In a form of protest, Yi collapsed to the floor in amongst the surrounding bodies. As for myself, I was at a loss about what to do in the echoes of an apparent pleasure palace. Without an immediate goal, leaving Yi in her inward state, I needed to take a walk, to catch my breath. As I moved about, I started to take a measure of the building, with its interconnecting walkways and complicated transport systems. Soon, I came across an auditorium, where again the same image from the atrium banner was on display. At once I knew what was required and made my way back to Yi.

Ensconced in the gathering of indoor sunbathers, and despite the cavernous acoustics of the hanger like hall, only a murmur sounded, nothing more. Yi and I lay together on the hard floor, basking in the glowing orb, staring down with all its might. The warm brush of orange cast upon a sea of multicoloured skins. In the mirrored ceiling we all looked like plankton, tourists in our own land. Yi was greatly comforted by what I had to report and we began to relax. We had time ahead of us.

'I love how the sun wants *nothing*', Yi whispered to me. 'It just goes on and on and on… Bet you can't do that!' she teased.

'What do you mean?' I asked, knowing full well.

'We are nothing, just stuff that comes streaming from the sun – mere spots in its glare. Flotsam and jetsam. It is not us who sees. It is the light that sees. I feel like we are on a boat somewhere. All these people are just tin cans bobbing about the surface. They can't see us. None of us *see* each other.'

Yi seemed amused by what she said – I less so. She reached across and placed her hand into my trousers. She knew I was already hard. She just held the shaft of my cock tight and didn't say a word more. A hot tickle of urine ran down between her legs. The flowing line burned into the concrete like a streak of black oil. We realised how hungry we were and agreed, before our plans for the evening, we really needed sustenance. We stood up and hand in hand stepped between the bodies. Spots of urine dissipated through the air as we made our way out. Yi laughed as she always did.

It was here in the heart of the city, at dusk, with the beginnings of rain dampening all the day's sun, that we were to hit hard up against the *scene that remains*. I see us. Yi places her right hand on my left arm to hold me back at that precise moment the traffic was very dense and energetic. She barely touched me, but softly spoke: 'pay attention *my love*'. I'm quite sure of it.

We had fallen into an unassuming restaurant in one of the back roads from the museum. We ordered copious amounts of oysters and lobster. Far more than we could possibly manage. Sat across from us, at the next table, was a straight-backed, elegantly coiffured woman. Her dark eyeliner and purply black lipstick appeared theatrical, yet defied her age, like a goddess or witch. In exquisite handwriting she had been making notes in several different notebooks at once, as if some elaborate musical score. But sentinel-like and quite feline in nature she slowly looked up on our arrival and gave a soft smile.

As we ate, Yi and I pulled closer, sitting next to each other from around the corner of the table. Yi gaily cracked the lobster claws to get each and every last piece of meat. I began to play with her underneath her dress. With the juices of the lobster and oysters streaming from her mouth, she kept muttering affirmatively, like a film I'd once watched, and repeating how good the nutrients of the lobster were for maintaining young, glowing skin. It was difficult to say if I was giving her the orgasm or if it was the food.

'Careful, *both* of you…' came the serene voice of the writer. Yi and I stopped abruptly, shocked the woman might have been able to see beneath the table.

'Don't worry', she said, laughing gently at our fright, 'you have nothing to hide. Besides, I can see around corners!'

Later, we kissed in Floral Street, except Yi never actually recalls, only ever smiles, still sorry about the rainwater down my back. Maybe this was the scene that remains. Our arms became our perimeter. I remember Yi's skin, the feel of her waist and we kept holding us, the tightness removing the need of fingerprints. I was talking, I was always talking, all of a sudden, I saw her gesture toward me, him her, us reflecting in the shop window – from around the umbrella she was clutching: *it was only gentle but it only needed to be so lightly and besides…*

We stopped talking: no defining line only rain coming down. I'm not sure how we kept our balance as the reflection of her came to him ever so lightly. Then a truck went passed and we over-stepped our places. I only remember the lamppost the noise of the wires of the umbrella and in the corner of my eye her-him, our reflection untying in the windowpane, as we escaped the scene I came to realize I was soaking all down my back. We laughed and Yi took my arm again; I barely noticed the dampness of my shirt and the cashmere droplets that continued to collect on the surface. I just stepped as neatly as I could by her side because Yi had soaked me through entirely.

Had I returned to the scene the next day I would have found the newly risen sun to have bleached out any traces of the steps we had taken. But this was the scene I took with me as we returned in the moonlight to the museum. At the back of the building, by a service entrance, we pushed at an unbarred window and cautiously climbed through. Without a flashlight it was difficult to make out anything. We were in a maze of narrow corridors with exposed pipes. We heard voices and both scattered, so becoming separated. After quietly calling out several times, but with no luck, I ventured on through what seemed like an endless warren. I cannot fully account for why I had the idea of first removing my trousers and continuing only in shirt and damp sweater. Yet, it was hot and humid, as if the pipes around me were all pumping steam. I removed all my clothes, piece by piece and placed them on a chair near a doorway. I had only my shoes on as I opened it and stepped suddenly and with great surprise back out to the atrium again. Its massiveness, seen now from the other end of the building, and completely devoid of people, was exhilarating. Yet, before I could fully breathe, I heard a rustling sound. Fearing I might be followed, I hurried through the various levels of the building to reach the auditorium, which was now thriving with guests and a panel of speakers upon a stage.

Nothing was more bizarre for me in that utterly thrilling moment than my nudity as I snuck into one of the back-row seats. Flushed face and out of breath I desperately looked about for Laura, but she was nowhere to be seen. The lights dimmed and a 'low budget' film began to play on multiple screens around the room. It gave a dizzying effect.

'Look!', someone blurted out. 'They are projecting the film from behind us'.

Spinning around to keep up with the motion of the camerawork I lost all sense of where I was — surely, I was at the centre of it all, and yet it was as if I'd been flung into *nowhere* with a centrifugal force. It was as if all reality were tearing apart: a hand, moistened by saliva, had grabbed my cock and was rubbing it. Thinking I had been sitting in the furthest most back row, I now discovered I was some way forward and a woman was reaching over from behind. Just at that moment — as the four video screens lit up in high contrast — my come shot up into what I could now see was the wonderful face of Yi.

'What did you do with your clothes?', I asked her, as we sunk limp in our seats.

She told me after we had split up, she undressed in order to 'feel more free'. The film finished and the lights in the auditorium came back up with a rush of applause. Yi was scanning the room anxiously, but we both knew the same: Laura was still nowhere to be seen. A panel of distinguished speakers now started talking and this went on for what was an inordinate length of time. They kept referring to Laura, some agreeing with her and others 'respectfully' taking a different view. 'There are those who use language to crucify meaning', began one woman, 'and those whose language creates'. This prompted a general murmur of agreement and led to concerns for the effects of writing taking the place of living. Following this a jovial man smoking a cigar spoke with great animation, his fingers dancing with every word. In what appeared a digression, he announced how Zeuxis had had the advantage by making grapes that attracted the birds. This, he went onto suggest, represented a 'triumph of the gaze over the eye'. A prim and proper looking man suggested that alongside the debate of voyeurism, 'it now seems surprising that little attention is paid to the complementary question of exhibitionism'. Later, another woman, who gave the disclaimer of only being able to speak as a physicist, returned repeatedly to the notion that while particles move in waves, they hit as particles, as things. She added how she was not sure what *it* was that particles hit against, when everything is evidently made up entirely of waves. She pondered we might all be living only on a single plane.

After we could bear no more, Yi and I slipped out unnoticed. The face on the banner in the foyer continued to stare as we walked away despondently. Yet all was not quite lost. As we looked up to a high walkway lined with glass, we saw the distinct figure of Laura. She was dressed head to toe in a dark cloak and around her was an escort of people in red blazers. They seemed to be hurrying somewhere. Laura caught sight of us far down in the atrium and the surprise seemed to restore life to her face. Yet, as we beckoned, she pulled a deep hood up over her head, sending her eyes into shadow. Yi, weeping almost, while I lovingly caressed her forehead, sent kisses, but it was too late. In that instant, Laura missed her footing and span into a shaken orbit. Those around her parried quickly and hastened to lead Laura away through a door. As she turned to look back in the final moment her face seemed no longer present. Through the glass we saw only what appeared to be a hooded mirror, the incidence of the moonlight casting sharply upon it.

Blood Line

It was pissing with rain as we left the city. The smell of sodden streets is associated for me with the rusty encrustations along the bottom of boats; and gun metal skylines, I hardly know why, with a limping dog that wandered about all alone on windy days outside a childhood holiday home. With the scenes of the 'cathedral' still playing in my mind, these polluting thoughts, or I should say, *sensations*, were connected in untold ways with the harrowed lines and strangely reflective glare upon Laura's face. But then, this clutter of pictures in my mind came over all speckled with blood spots, first like dark raindrops, then bleached marks as can scar rushes of film. I thought back further. Laura could come only by soaking herself, not with blood I hasten to add, but with chaotic streams of urine that, while spurting and spitting at first, would ease to a hot trickle and then with the hushed sound of utter relief. I had to believe that even the *bleakest and most leprous aspects of a dream are merely an urging in that direction, an obstinate waiting for total joy.* The scene upon that glass-lined walkway whereupon Laura tottered must surely lead somewhere.

But then and there, in the spitting rain, Yi and I had been forced to flee like two weak birds. Cold and dejected, we made our way back to the train station. We had managed to pilfer black trench coats, which, despite still going barefoot, gave us sufficient cover to board the next train out of the city. Having returned to the 'real world', *the one made up solely of dressed people*, we slumped into our seats and watched the platform slide away. We neither spoke, nor looked at one another. Despite all that had passed, we felt strangely satisfied being there together, the world moving around us; all wrapped into oneness, all the lewdness, weariness and absurdity was held there in our silence, unseen by anyone, unless looking through our very eyes, or tracing directly our memories.

As the train began to pick up speed we drifted in and out of consciousness. Indeed, we were perishingly fatigued. We sweated and shivered variously, and against the cold window of the carriage we tried to gain the warmth of our combined bodies. Yi, however, was beginning to exhibit a particular indisposition. I tried to comfort her, yet she trembled all over and chattered her teeth. I suggested I might be able to find some food in one of the further compartments, but this only made things worse. The very thought of eating led Yi to frequent the washroom numerous times. Finally, she returned to her seat ready to settle again. She looked haggard and deathly white. Kissing me as if to thank me for my patience (even though all I was able to do was wait anxiously), I caught that faint whiff of butyric acid.

Several days later I received the telephone call. It must have been not long after dawn. I scarcely kept upright to get to the receiver. When I did, in that instance, I stopped breathing. It was Yi. We never called one another, there was never any need. Yet now, suddenly, in isolation was just her voice; something that looking back I realise I had rarely ever heard without equally seeing her beautiful face and feeling her skin. I adjusted to the abstraction and the compression of the line (*the sound of distance suppressed*), I soon learnt the true meaning of the call. A kaleidoscopic proximity ensued as I realised I was both 'there' talking to Yi, yet miles, hours away from her. She was in the hospital she told me.

My agitation grew in not knowing what to do. I could hardly put the telephone down (in order to rush to her), yet neither could I seem to find anything sensible to say.

'Don't go,' she said, tremulously.

Taking hold of myself, I told her I'd come right away, but she begged me not to hang up. The nurses would be back to look after her very soon she explained and that there was not time for me to reach her.

'Yi! Yi!' I called plaintively, hopelessly. I wanted to kiss her I told her, but I could not tell if she heard; all we had were our voices like ghosts.

'Speak to me,' I continued, but Yi was no longer to be heard. Instead, I listened to muffled voices and perhaps the faint sound of something metallic. Like the sensation of feeling through the dark I called Yi's name and tried to ask what was happening. Nothing came back. My mind was racing and strangely enough, without thinking it, I returned to the very first instance I thought I'd never see Yi again, when we all waved goodbye, on the night she climbed out the car with her crutches.

Whether it was the stress of the situation or something else, I do not know, but with the receiver still pressed hard to my ear with one hand, with the other I clamped hold of my severe erection. My trousers at my knees, I masturbated violently – so much harder than I had ever done so before. Rage swelled as much as my penis distended and ballooned. Tears formed around my eyes, making them globular and heavy. My semen seeded over the base of the telephone and mixed around my fingers.

The contradiction of what had inevitably been my prolonged state of exhaustion and the absurd rigidity of my penis was all bound up with my presence on the telephone line. Yi, of course, was witness to none of this and I too was soon transported to her side as her voice, croaky and weak, came back to life. I felt as if I could almost see her as she spoke. Indeed, to this day, when I replay this scene, I am sitting next to her and can picture as clear as anything the blue hospital gown and her matted hair. I see her eyes aglow, peering back constantly despite the fatigue as she tells me everything is over, that she has been given a sedative and told to rest. As her voice fades with the effects of the medication her voice grows husky and, indistinctly, I think I hear her say goodbye.

I found her inert, her mouth half-open against the pillow, her gown open. Traced through her panties, the length of her labia, ran a thin line of clotted blood. Terrified, I took hold of her hand, but her whole arm fell limp from the bed. I then threw myself upon her, scooping her up in my arms, shaking through my whole body, and as I held her there tightly, I was overcome with spasms, tears and drool.

It took a moment to realise, but Yi was slowly coming

to: her hand reached out to mine involuntarily, and I pulled back to take in the sight of her whole body now reviving. I was ecstatic to see life return to what I had thought was Yi's corpse, but I quickly took to admonishing her for playing such a trick on me. She told me not to make her laugh as it hurt, but happily there not a mark or bruise upon her. I took her in my arms and carried her as far and quickly from the hospital as I could, regardless of any sense of fatigue and debility. I had left as early as I could and now the antelucan mist was breaking into morning sunshine. Fuelled only by adrenalin, I rushed with superhuman effort to reach Yi's house and took absolute pride in placing my dear amazing friend, very much alive and trembling like a flower, into her own bed.

It was then that my all-encompassing enervation fully overcame me. I was sweating, my eyes bleary, my body shivering, and my head and heart throbbed deep within as if the blood coursing through my veins was still believing me to be running. But since *I had just rescued the person I loved most in the world*, and since I thought we would soon be seeing Laura, I fell next to Yi just as I was, perspiring in my ragged clothes, and drifted in and out of hectic dreams.

Time-lapse

One of the most peaceful times for me was the period of Yi's convalescence. The days were warm, but not too hot. I read books in fragments, tossed through newspapers, and listened idly to an FM radio on low.

It surely goes without saying the subject of eggs no longer came up in our conversation, *with one exception*, and certainly we never played with them again. From that time on, if we happened to see an egg in each other's company we would generally avert our gaze and a silence would transform all sense of time, or if our eyes did meet it would yield what I can only describe as a 'murky interrogation'. I shall return to the matter before this tale is through, when it will be evident this interrogation was not without its proper answer.

Yi mostly stayed in bed, drifting in and out of sleep. I sat by her side occasionally reading out loud some of the more outré items of news. As required, I would help her in her feverish state to reach the bathroom so she could pee, or to help her bathe. Yi was extremely weak during these days and while we would entangle ourselves, naturally I never stroked her. Instead, we became engrossed in a new obsession.

I had managed to procure a computer and monochrome monitor, which I duly set up in perfect eye-line with Yi's reclined figure. I ran a long cable to the hallway in order to reach the telephone socket. I had to switch out the plug for the household telephone, which caused come consternation, but it would be days at a time before this would be found out.

At first everything was text-based. Sometimes, when Yi lay sleeping, I indulged in playing text adventure games. I never tired of watching writing scroll upon the screen and I was enthralled with how you could traverse the landscape of these words, typing commands to 'go north' or 'enter room'. Yet, I always got stuck in one particular place. I never could fathom how to get passed the repeating phrase of 'pale bulbous eyes'. They were supposedly spiders, but all I had to go by was the same line scrolling up the screen, 'pale bulbous eyes'. There was no way to rid of them. If you tried to evade them the game would end. Counter-intuitively, and only years later, I learnt the way to escape was to 'wait' several times on the spot, surrounded by them, and then move on.

Together, Yi and I discovered a surfeit of message boards and chatrooms. We made up fantasies and pretended to be older than we really were. A couple of times we panicked and thought we might be found out, so we pulled the cable from the socket. But it soon became clear there was little if no comeback. We would likely have tired of the computer by this point, but it was our discovery of a young woman alone in her bedroom that really changed things and when our obsession kicked in. We never knew her name, which maybe helped in part for her to stand in as a surrogate for Laura. Yi and I referred to her simply as 'the girl'. We no longer needed to type, but instead watched an endless sequence of images, each drawing slowly on the screen, replacing the one before, though always punctured with an abrupt black screen, clearing the way for the next to incrementally reveal itself line by line, progressively filling the pitch-dark frame. In this way the daily activities of the girl were cut into single frames, updating only *every three minutes*. Whatever may have happened between each picture would remain unseen and so, as much as each image performed its own little striptease, the sequence from one to the next ran in a kind of collaged slow-motion.

The girl became our constant companion. At the regular intervals of each frame she might be at her computer doing homework, or siting on the bed flicking through channels (the faint glow of the television screen apparent upon her face). Other times she might paint her nails, try on outfits, sleep, eat food out of bowls, or do her make-up wearing a headband. She would dance too. And sometimes, she seemed to do nothing but stare, and it would appear to Yi and I that what she looked like related to what she saw.

This went on *every three minutes*, for hours at a time. On a few occasions the girl performed 'shows' dressed up in garter belts and spike heels. These scenes led Yi to daydream about holding Laura, similarly in garter-belt and stockings (and nothing else), with legs bent, head down and vulva protruding. Yi herself, in soaking clothes, would expose her breasts, which, between finger and thumb, I would arouse from afar by spinning the focal ring of a single-lens reflex camera that had just fired its flash (first startling us, and secondly giving out a pungent smell of magnesium from the spent bulb). At the same time, she would lick her finger, placing it in Laura's anus while freely peeing in her dress and onto Laura's back. I'd urinate over them both from the other side, and should she wish, she'd stick my cock in her mouth, and so on and so on.

These such dreams would meld with our viewing of the monitor screen, with its own oneiric rhythm of swiping and re-writing the screen. Through this undulating time-lapse, we once watched the girl undress with her boyfriend, but this was not nearly as fascinating as just watching her stare back at us. An erotics of the body comes where the garment gapes, so someone said. The camera was a window, and it was when it seemed near to shatter that we were most drawn in.

'Do you think people would look at me the way we look at her, if I were not with you?' Yi asked.

A little unsettled, I only replied: 'Have you noticed how she is happier, lighter, after she has applied her make-up?'

'Yet she can't see us,' Yi laughed, 'it is not the make-up that lifts her mood, which makes her look like her mother, it is getting the mirror to notice'.

Yi's capacity to be alone had never crossed my mind before. But during this time she began to vocalise the wish not to be left by herself. She was quite capable of being alone when I was present, she said, but she did not like it when I had to leave the sanctum of the bedroom – whether it was to go to the market, or even just to take some fresh air and look across at the shoreline. As a result, Yi declared she wanted a camera of her own. It will feel like a 'little buddy' she had said. Of course, I was required to duly leave the bedroom only to then return with the little spherical device, which we attached to the top of the computer screen.

As children we had been told not to make an exhibition of ourselves (*'arrête ton cinéma!'*), yet now, placing the camera upon ourselves was more akin to holding up a magnifying glass. It brought us closer and allowed us to explore a whole new terrain of our bodies and their sensations. Given this period of slow recuperation, it meant we could barely touch one another, yet we reached whole new heights of affection. Sometimes, gently rubbing Yi, she would drift into a half state of both feeling my fingers, yet also spying upon herself via the screen. She liked me to keep my eyes on her image, just to make sure it was certainly there.

'Look at me! Look at me!' she would cry, by which I knew she meant for me to keep my eyes upon the window of the screen, to look outwardly so as to look in. Of course, for all my explanation of what happened during these days we never spoke of what we did or what we saw, we never gave commentary. *Our originary form of address was, and remains* (in memory), *essentially mute.*

As it happened, I chanced upon a review in one of the newspapers, offering its well-to-do audience some deeper explanation of the goings on of the girl on cam. The camera, it described, 'might seem an unlikely confidant. With its circular lens set in a white sphere it resembles an eyeball'. The article proceeded to suggest that our 'apparent assumption that the gaze is fundamentally benign cannot be based on the evidence of history, or the testimony of the contemporary news media', nor apparently our own experience, and yet somehow, the author held out, it might be a consequence of something that was for all intents and purposes 'good enough'.

At night-time, as Yi and I drifted to sleep, all bundled up, a collection of limbs and flesh, moonlight cast upon the bedroom picking out the little camera upon the computer screen. Its bulbous eye, like an alien egg, kept open its interrogation, the unexpected answer to which, perhaps, was always necessary *for measuring the immensity of the void that yawned before us,* without our knowledge, as during that time in which we now no longer pursued those singular entertainments with the eggs.

Laura

As already mentioned, Yi and I rarely talked about our obsessions. We never spoke of the interest we had in one another, and still less about what Laura meant to us. Nonetheless, and despite our compulsive use of the computer during Yi's confinement (our idée fixe with the monitor screen), we never stopped looking forward to the next occasion when we could go back to Laura. Nothing seemed plainer than the prospect of having her live with us in Yi's room secretly along with me.

Over a month went by before Yi could travel again. As before, we took the train to the city, though this time we took care to remain inconspicuous. It gave me little pleasure to return to the 'cathedral' of art, my dread due in part perhaps to the association of *cathedrae molles*, or maybe the learned sense, that of the professor's chair (which, as we shall see, proved prophetic). Yet, worse, we arrived to find the great big building closed; the early signs of dereliction creeping in. Hung over the front entrance was a sign marked crudely on cardboard, fluttering in the wind.

This setback, however, was not as stark as we had first feared. Across the road, a man, standing in the doorway of a second-hand bookshop, its windows yellow with a protective film, beckoned us over. He listened carefully and thoughtfully as we told our strange tale. When we had finished, he simply laughed and told us we were looking in the wrong place. Instead, he directed us to the heart of the city, telling us to take this road then that, until eventually we would reach the university library. There we would find Laura. He was emphatic on this point.

After threading our way through the city for nearly an hour, and then finally evading security, we entered the library and strode purposefully to the front desk. We announced that we had come to find Laura, that we'd been told it was the right place. The young man behind the counter looked quizzically at us before disdainfully gesturing to a row of computers.

'You can find things on the catalogue,' he said flatly, 'just type in your search. It'll tell you where you need to go'.

With that he handed us a cheaply photocopied leaflet with a map of the numerous floors of the library, all marked out with strange coding of numbers and letters.

The bank of computer terminals was placed across an impressive wooden standing desk, the sort of thing where you might romantically imagine scribes of a bygone age working upon their illuminated manuscripts. Yi took delight in waking up all of the screens before settling at one of them.

'Where… is… Laura…?', Yi sounded out as she typed one finger at a time.

However, upon hitting return nothing intelligible came back. She tried numerous times, and with several variations. All to no avail: 'No Match' was all we were told. Fortunately, the young librarian had been hovering behind us. He had watched with a wry smile and now intervened.

'You can't ask it direct questions like that,' he explained, 'it's too many variables'.

In saying so, he demonstrated. Typing our one precious name the computer spat out a series of codes. These, he explained, where locations upstairs in the library and he circled things hurriedly on our map.

The entrance to the library proper was without ostentation. It was merely the entrance to a staircase, with a sign above the doorway: 'To the Library'. We climbed up many flights, stopping off at each of the floors without really knowing where we were heading. The map bore little resemblance to the irregularity and creakiness that lay behind each of the connecting doors. Despite the impressive size and severity of the tower as seen from outside, with its aura of regimented neoclassicism, and of near totalitarian scale, the interior was a warren of shabby and claustrophobic passageways, endless bookshelves and scattered reading rooms. Floors were uneven, steps went up in places, only to drop down again to enter rooms, and furniture and fittings were idiosyncratic, battered and strained with years of use. One constant, however, was the strong odour of stagnation and mould. Nothing terrifying.

We were soon quite lost. Here and there we noticed individuals sitting at desks consulting books, or more often slumped over their papers. In amongst all the books, stored on shelves as far as one could see, all coded yet easily forgotten, I was struck by the calm and serenity. The students we saw, and the occasional professors, seemed to sit lost in their own worlds like patients in a sanatorium. They were quite oblivious to our presence; their long-term indisposition was to pour over these books, as if for centuries and centuries, hoping one day to violate all the secrets. I have read somewhere that the scribes of the Middle Ages tired of only copying, and instead wanted to produce new works, *impelled by the lust for novelty*; and that since then learning is not like a token that remains physically whole as if infinitely exchangeable. Instead, it is more like a dress, worn out and sullied through use. Books themselves are like this, their pages crumble and inks fade with time with too many hands upon them. Is this the reason for the 'lust for novelty' – our attempt to keep all this alive? We simply write more and longer so to keep all of this from crumbling.

I had the sense the library was breathing in and out. I felt it quite palpably. Upon the shelves and desks and as held deep between the pages of the books were all the years of saliva, nasal excretions, breath, sweat, ear wax, food, coffee, come and the grime of millions of fingernails. It was all here. Yet nowhere could we find Laura.

At this point Yi came over quite faint. It was the first time she had been away from her bedroom for any length of time, and we had had little to eat or drink. I helped her into a chair next to two students who were simultaneously playing a game of snakes and ladders and a match of chess. The exalted tossing of the dice for the one, seemed to clash with the strained ponderings of the other. They did not seem to mind Yi groaning quietly next to them and I took the opportunity to seek their advice.

Fortunately, they were able to give us a definite destination, an office somewhere in the outer university buildings. First, of course, we had to get out of the library, which was baffling. We took the first set of stairs going down, only to find we arrived higher up, where the tower narrowed, and the passageways grew dimmer. We started our descend again. We passed desks of individuals we thought we'd seen before, but could never be quite sure, though strangely we never did see again the two students playing snakes and ladders. Eventually we fell through a side door, out into the city, gasping for air and feeling the joy of sunlight. I recall it being said we are always concerned with how we might get out of a labyrinth, but perhaps the question is where does it even begin? This was now our next problem as we traversed the various buildings in search of Laura.

Eventually the moment came. We were face to face with what we had been told was the door of Laura's office. Unlike the other offices along the corridor there was no name plate, and before I could knock Yi simply strode in. There in front of us, surrounded by untold papers and files, was Laura. She looked up in total bewilderment. As she stood up, we rushed to embrace her. Laura hardly seemed to recognise us and stood like an unsure animal in our arms; she flinched when I tried to kiss her. As we stood there silently, a faint trickle of liquid was heard as Laura peed straight onto her flat-heeled shoes. She gazed into mid-air, and seemed occupied by relentless, yet unconnected thoughts.

'Doctor,' she yelled, 'let me know when you're done fucking my wife!'

In this split second all the demoralising effects of our having been parted from Laura hit to the core. We tried to steady her as she collapsed back into the chair. Yi knelt beside her, her eyes welling up. She curled her arms around Laura's legs. At first, she only brushed her cheek against the thigh, but then, a surge of passion took hold of her. Yi spread Laura's legs apart, and, pressing her lips to Laura's, greedily devoured.

Yi and I still had to comprehend the fact that Laura grasped nothing of what was going on. She was incapable of telling one thing from another. She was quite unaware of Yi's existence, batting her away at one point having mistaken her for a cat on account of her black hair and because she appeared to be sat upon her lap, docilely rubbing and caressing like a contented feline. Yet, when I asked Laura about the 'cathedral' she understood it was the place that had carried her away. In terror she hunched up like a little girl having witnessed something unspeakable. I looked upon her with unease and since my gaze was taut and inscrutable, I only frightened her further, leading her to snap back.

'I look, I see…' she cried out, as if reprimanding us both, 'The room offers itself to me in its nakedness'.

It was now dark outside and the office was lit by faint moonlight. Yi and I were exhausted from our travels, but we wanted so much to take Laura back with us, to take care of her.

'But which room do you see?' Yi asked her.

'The room through the keyhole,' said Laura.

'And what do you see?' I added.

Laura was in and out of lucidity, and spoke as if transfixed, an automaton:

'I've been looking at these pictures for so long… but we were never really there… just the scenery…'

Slowly, Yi and I were coming to realise that Laura referred to her time, many times, being in the wardrobe, looking out. It had been her eye that looked out at us, but we had never stopped to think what she saw coming in; of all the vicariousness bestowed upon her. Even the vacant room, after all our debaucheries were done, looked back at her.

Yet, Laura's terror was not what she had seen, but rather

the endless demand, the unabated hunger, to recreate the scenes in her imagination, and more so the fact that this evaded her again and again. The time she was driven to the beach in the wardrobe was a long, slow haulage, like the twisting and pulling of an implement from a wound; she was pulled not struck out of a dreamscape, the intensities all draining from the scene, never to be seen again. Desperate to invent details, over and over, she put herself into the most inviting positions. Yet, no, this was not true. My words are all dead to me. We stood in our huddle, yet each untouched, *powerless to affect the intensity of what was.*

(Open Eyes of) Vertigo

We sat quite still after our sudden discovery. We were helpless in the realisation of what we had precipitated. We cradled Laura in our arms, as if asleep, as if a life-like doll. Her tight-fitting trousers and high-neck top encased her, as ever, keeping her millimetres apart from us. Except one of her sleeves was torn, exposing the grey, parchment-like flesh of her upper arm. As if looking at the world through a lens I couldn't tell if Laura was falling away from me, or if I was pulling apart from her. Her face was obscured by her hair, yet, still, there she was in my arms. *We didn't dare budge, and all we desired was for that unreal immobility to last as long as possible*, and for Laura to fall sound asleep. In what felt like hours, but was only minutes, *my mind reeled in some kind of exhausting vertigo*. I felt little tremors of doubt and guilt.

For a short period, Yi and I saw less of each other. She had retreated again to her bedroom, staying up all hours watching the world through the window of the computer. She still had the little camera set up to record her own room at random intervals. While claiming she had no idea when or if it was recording, I caught her a few times showing off to it. But, worse, the final time I logged on, I saw only Yi's torso and parts of her limbs, which trailed off into the bedclothes; her head was cut off from the shot. She must have been sleeping, but through the lens appeared what seemed the rump of a cadaver, and cuttingly, staring back at me, was the decisive 'V' of her sex. I felt ashamed to see her in this way, as if through a letterbox, a peepshow.

It was during this time I met K. and for all its brevity took solace in this new friendship. She was already a famous singer before I came to know her, and truth be told I was quite enamoured. Yet, we never spoke of who we were. I admired her carefree way (despite everything in her life being controlled) and she was protective of me, aware of the deep sadness in my eyes.

In taking a break from the intensity of Yi's seclusion, I had found some causal work at a TV studio, running errands, sitting on the set when the crew broke for lunch, that sort of thing. On occasion I was summoned to dressing rooms to collect or deliver something. The day I entered *her* dressing room seemed no different to any other. Like any other star, she sat before a large mirror, a make-up artist working upon her face. I left a plate of food discretely upon the dresser, but K. stopped me.

'Hey,' she said in a nasally tone, 'where you going? That is really kind.'

I told her it was no problem and thought it my cue to

leave but found myself pulled into a conversation that would stretch over much of the summer. On that particular day, as the make-up artist stepped back to admire her creation, K. let out a pleasurable groan and gushed forth with praise. She jumped up and looked me straight in the eye.

'Come on, I need you to do something! Do you know how to take pictures?'

We ran about the studio complex finding unusual places for her to pose. K. took delight in running down steps or looking back over her shoulder. I took picture after picture. This was how our friendship began. She loved the photographs, taking delight in what I had seen. I always felt disappointed. The moment the camera shutter engages something changes; particles elide. K. never saw the beauty I saw. Yet, she enjoyed her own image, uninhibited. Over the course of several months, whenever possible, I would join her backstage, travelling as part of her entourage. We staged many more impromptu photoshoots (just for the fun of it, just to evade the day's schedule); we played board games to kill time, we shared food, and often fell asleep in the lulls between rehearsals. More than anything, K. taught me the importance of her 'looks divine', because otherwise we are so hard to see.

Thinking back, I learnt all this in a single instance, that very first day. It happened the moment she was up on stage as the lights went down and the filming began. Looking up from below, less than an arm's length away (an extra in the adoring crowd), my vision spiralled into her as she lip-synched a song. I realised then I was looking *through* her; nothing comes before the possibility of prosthetic iterability. *Before I look*: there is already the operation *of selection, of exposure time, of filtering, of development*. Unless, of course, there was in fact nothing there; 'I can see right through you', I could hear Laura say.

But, in that instance, I understood the wonder of what it was to be *mythical*. K. belongs to a time when it is less the human face than the figure that plunges an audience into the deepest ecstasy, when one supposedly loses oneself in the pin-up image as one might the callings of a dance floor, where the body offers a kind of absolute state of being, which can be neither touched nor relinquished.

It was indeed an admirable body-object, *spinning around*, the fetish of the camera surrounding her diminutive *derrière*. Yet, it was less the lithe body thrust upon her audience than the whole of the figure she sung with that drew me close. From between her high-glossed lips and disproportionally large teeth came a thin, nasally voice supremely suited to the cloned multitrack. And had I mistaken her for her own waxwork, the *signs* were all of a red-blooded woman whose breathy asides syncopated with the music; with ease letting slip a Monroe-like temptation, 'so now, shall I remove my clothes…?'

Despite its singular beauty, her body, posed yet lived as something free and staged, that is, both flighty and poised, acted out a succession of feminine forms (yet always as herself). What I learnt, without ever knowing it, was that K. negotiates the gaze as a play between lovers; no one is made to feel guilty. And K. was no drag act: she revelled in her sensuality upon the stage; all pronounced with humour. Her deliberate play of glamour less the affectation of beauty than the airing of its genealogy, namely those heavenly stars of yesteryear we only know from the pure light of the silver screen. Looking down from the stage, the singer knew she was not her Name any more than the heroines she evoked. Barefoot and lolling about the beach, Bardot was known to say of appearing before the camera: 'I am myself'. For K. it was the articulation of just such a role:

'I change characters when I do a photo shoot,' she would say to me, 'it's kind of avoiding being me – which I've become very good at.'

And yet, through this adored body was something rarer than a performance; a fantastical, bi-vocal gesture *flying in the languages of style /stealing from the languages of style, making them fly*. A performance gives the pleasure of something we cannot reproduce for ourselves; an embodiment, on the contrary, activates pleasure without separation, as *jouissance*. Up there, an alien form (or so she was described), K. was at once intimate yet strange; a mannequin leaning towards her audience, delivering each of us in turn a secret smile, letting the seductions of the flesh as code yield its place to an *écriture* of Woman.

Through the many figures of K. that I would witness through the camera lens and upon the stage, oscillated two iconographic ages, which many years later I understood to go from awe to charm: from the face of Garbo as aura, to the event of Hepburn (a delectable interplay of idiosyncrasies). Yet something else prevailed: the youthful erotics of detachment. The movie screen created the lascivious Bardot, yet the lens never tamed her indifference and ambiguity. I've heard it said: 'her eroticism is not magical, but aggressive.' Today, the rightful heir is the supermodel whose body never flinches and declares nothing. If K. was alien, the supermodel was unassailable. In her body language, K. always exuded frankness, of the order of *drawing*, that of the supermodel only the order of photography. The body of K. was about play, that of the other, surrender. Of course, despite these reveries, I was always aware the halcyon days of my summer hiatus would be short lived. Although, I might remark, throughout this time I never once thought to express myself sexually. It was as if I had returned, temporarily, to my younger days with feverish, yet downcast eyes.

I will merely report here that Laura died of exposure, the full tragic circumstances of which might never be known. She recognised the imaginal economy she had spied for us all, making visible that which could not be seen. Yet this incarnation, like the Holy Trinity, could never be an in-corporation, only ever an in-imagination. Like the smile of the long-dead queen that continues to reproduce itself upon the many surviving portraits, we are left only with absolute, theoretical vision. We see only what we look at. That is all that is left of us. That is what Laura knew when she returned to the edge of the cliff, looking out to the infinite horizon of the sea. When she stepped forth, I can only think, for an instance, she believed in the Image (our ability to imagine) as infinite. Yet infinity must be present *all at once*. While we can *potentially* count numbers infinitely, this action nonetheless takes place over time. It was just such a cut in time that saw Laura plummet to the sandy beach below.

By the time we had reached her, she was quite dead. The sun and sea had drained all colour from the skin and there was only a faint rotting, sweet fragrance in the air. Noticing I was aroused, Yi began tossing me off. I stretched out in the sand, it was impossible not to; *Yi was still a virgin, and I fucked her for the first time next to the corpse.* It was very painful, yet we were glad precisely because it *was* painful. When we had finished, we looked down at the corpse. Laura was now a stranger, and in fact, to me, so was Yi. My love for them both had seemed to evaporate. Or perhaps it was me that had died another little death. It would have been of little surprise; all was so strange. I watched Yi, and recall quite vividly, the only sensations I truly felt came from the filthy things she was doing to the corpse. It irritated her, *as though she could not bear the thought that this creature, so similar to her, could not feel her anymore.* The open eyes irritated her the most. Even after drenching the face, *those eyes, extraordinarily, did not close.* The calmness of all *three* of us was perhaps the most despairing part of it. All the boredom in the world I connect to this moment and to the great betrayal of death. All of which does not stop me from thinking back with revulsion, and, if I'm honest, abetment. It is just that the lack of excitement made it all the more absurd, and thus *Laura was closer to me dead than in her lifetime.* The fact Yi dared piss on the corpse (whether out of boredom or, more troublingly, in irritation): it merely reminds of our refusal and inability to understand what was happening. Of course, it is no more understandable today than it was back then.

Delicacies of the Cock

To avoid the bother of a police investigation, we made plans to head to Shanghai. Yi said we could lie low with an English professor who had always made clear their unconditional support and shelter. Years before, they had sat in a bar late one-night speaking of the ethics of cities. They looked her straight in the eye:

'If I asked you to do something, no questions asked, you'd do it', they had declared.

They watched Yi's hesitation, her youthful instinct to equivocate. Feeling she had immediately broken the promise with her split-second wavering, Yi responded affirmatively, though fearing all was lost.

'You would do it. I trust you', they confirmed, offering a wink. 'That is what I mean about the city', they went on, 'it gives harbour to these little narratives, these incidents'. It was the first time Yi drank brandy.

Yi's only means of contact was an old pager, but she was convinced they would show. We looked out from the large windows of the Pearl Tower restaurant. Slowing turning in its ovoid dome, watching the tugboats silently drifting around the arch of the waterway, you could be forgiven for thinking you are staring out at the banks of the Thames. Yi had left a cryptic message, asking if her Mephistopheles might do her one last favour: a grand favour. As we sat there, stationary yet moving, I couldn't help feeling the pangs of nausea that now dogged me. It was not *inside* me, but *out there*, across at the other beautifully laid tables, behind the bar with its allure of countless spirits, and down in the streets across the river (with all manner of diversity sloping in and out).

When it was time, we headed down to the nearby station. I put in earphones to drown out all that surrounded me; Yi marched along, a mute, animated doll. No sooner had we arrived I felt the nudge of her elbow and saw her delight and relief: Like a rock star ascending the Professor came up through the underground entrance. They had an unmistakable look of knowing, of charm. Dressed in a Teddy Boy suit and suede creepers, a tie flapping out of their pocket, they had surely not been to bed the night before. They knew what they had to do, *like the guitar licking that sidles up, shimmies off, and with the second refrain a foot beneath thump of boot, paused adjust*, the Professor hit the autumn sunshine *like the snares that beat in rattle*, now as they walked, *the hi-hats fizzed* in time with their stride, *the tension holding flicking tombola*, and yes, their smile said it all: 'This time, I know we could get it together… If I did causally mention tonight… That would be crazy to-night'.

The sun setting, we made our way through the narrow lanes of the old part of town. Passing noddle bars and tea houses, we eventually came upon the incongruity of an old English pub due for demolition. It was fenced in but stood distinctively as a perfect copy of a traditional village pub. We pushed passed bamboo scaffold and fencing to enter a small beer garden. A sign swung in the evening breeze as if nothing had changed. The Sun Inn: A big orange ball depicted on a silhouetted landscape. The clear, neat graphics were out of keeping with the sleepy, gabbled building. The Professor quietly played with the lock and soon we were inside, the glare of the street's neon signs now only tracing through a latticed window. The light glanced across a tatty pool table. Blunt-ended cues lay upon the table as if mid-game, yet the place had long been shut up. The odour of dampness, old beer and piss lingered, but everywhere was thick with dust and mice ran about the sticky floor.

Bone-weary from our travels and the sheer weight of everything, Yi and I looked about desperately for somewhere to sleep. But the Professor was having none of it. Salvaging an old chalkboard from behind the bar, they insisted we walk through every little detail of Laura's death while they made copious notes and drew diagrams and sketches. Making little sense to us, they spoke rapidly and excitedly of a lure of the screen, of a backward glance, of the 'field of the visible'. Finally, having exhausted the full extent of the board with a wild mixture of algebraic symbols, arrows and dotted lines, the Professor stood back in satisfaction.

'I must insist,' they announced, 'in the scopic field, the gaze is outside, I am looked at; that is to say, I am a picture'.

At this point they erased everything upon the board and promptly drew the outline of a body according to the dimensions as best we knew. They then lay the picture upon the floor and asked Yi to re-enact everything she had done to the corpse, to urinate upon the figure's face, upon those stubborn open eyes. During all this, the Professor never once touched her.

However, there had been a definite change in Yi. She would frequently stare into space, and I missed her constant chatter. It was as if she belonged away from this world – a world that seemed only to bore her. If she did exhibit her usual animation it was upon the occasions of seeing herself in mirrors (of which previously she had paid little attention). Or it was purely by way of orgasms. While these were rare, they were incomparably more violent than before. These orgasms were as different from normal climaxes as, say, the mirth of savage pornographies, with all parts of the body offering up violent release; with those involved 'whirling willy-nilly, flailing their arms about wildly, shaking their bellies, necks, and chests, and chortling and gulping horribly'. As for Yi, *she would first open uncertain eyes, at some lewd and dismal sight…*

For example, the next morning, at the crack of dawn, the Professor took us to a market. Stall owners were touting their wares: all manner of thick chunks of meats, vast arrays of fish (their eyes gleaming in the rising sun), and rows upon rows of buckets and trays of slimy, translucent sea creatures. We passed a myriad of cages with live and copulating species: Snakes of all hues, beavers, badgers, bats, civet cats, foxes, peacocks, porcupines, and pangolins. Taking refuge in a darkly lit tea shop, itself a bizarre emporium of animals and antiques, with a musty, leafy aroma, Yi grabbed hold of me and had me fuck her on and on, across a thousand-year-old gnarled rosewood table. The Professor sat beside us and jerked off. Kicking away from me, Yi grabbed her own arse and threw herself head-first, banging violently against the ground. Breathless, yet undeterred, she buried her fingernails into her buttocks, before thrashing about like a headless chicken, before stunning herself with a heavy thud against a terracotta statue. The Professor thrust their wrist into Yi's mouth, letting her bite hard to allay the spasm that kept shaking her, and I saw her face smeared with saliva and blood. Outside, in cages hanging from the rafters, two miner birds copied the various shrieks and gasps. After these fits, Yi always sought comfort in my arms, remaining huddled up like a little girl; solemn, still, and silent.

In the unfolding days, the Professor delved deep to sate our needs with all number of random salacious acts, yet Yi preferred only to eat. On entering a restaurant off from the market, she stood in great fascination, as had become her way, simply watching our food being prepared. Holding a chicken by its legs, its head naturally pushing out like a man's throbbing cock, the cook – in one deft slice – drained the blood about his feet, as the bird flopped about uncannily. Pouring vodka across the neck, he then dipped the whole bird briefly in a barrel of boiling water before thrusting it into a rotator that drew off the feathers with a flicking and spitting sound. The cook quickly and quietly splayed the bird, made little slits around its feet, and cut down to the groin. He sliced upwards towards the breast, before pulling the whole of the skin over the head, to hang off like a coat. Next, he removed the head, and, making sure not to disrupt the organs, especially the intestines, he cut deep from the groin, allowing the organs simply to slip out. Yi's heart throbbed when a little bladder dropped out, exploding its urine in one quick plop.

Less than half an hour later, the whole chicken – head to toe – was placed before us in a huge steaming pot. Large red chillies swam about the surface of the bubbling hot broth. Yi stood up, her face brimming with excitement. She never failed to express total joy at the sight of food. Snapping up the long server's chopsticks, she proceeded to give a hearty stir. She took in a deep breath, letting the full aroma in and then letting out a low moan of appreciation. She fished about purposefully. She was searching for something and soon found it. She pulled out an eel-like piece of flesh that seemed almost alive between her chopsticks.

'Give it to your young man here,' the Professor said with a broad smile. 'This is the stuff of virility. You will appreciate it later tonight', they laughed. They went on to cite how, in many cultures, where the body is thought of as a set of separate animated parts, 'cocks are viewed as detachable, self-operating penises, ambulant genitals with a life of their own'.

But Yi was not listening. Instead, she stared intently at the glistening flesh and dripping beads of soup. She was enthralled with this little piece of cartilage, which she landed proudly in a small porcelain bowl.

'This is mine,' she said, beaming, 'the top of the cock!'

Flung Ink

On the afternoon of the fourteenth a delegation of Parisian intellectuals arrived in Shanghai. The weather was warm and grey, with a few drops of rain. Their arrival had been reported in the local newspaper. Among the group was an avant-garde novelist of some repute. He was now nearing his forties, but handsome, and going by his photograph retained a certain mischief. Yi had been drawn to his picture, and, unusually perhaps, showed genuine enthusiasm when the Professor suggested we join the group's chaperoned tour of the city.

We reached the hotel in the English district in time for breakfast and quickly ingratiated ourselves. One member of the group stood out from the rest. Somewhat older, with the look of the philosopher about him, he sat adrift. He was slow and reluctant in his deportment. He smoked continually with a pensive or perhaps just a bored look upon his face. On the terrace beyond the breakfast room could be seen a solitary man lazily exercising. The philosopher looked upon him calmly, engulfed in his smoke while sipping tea. He muttered quietly: 'No muscles, no bones either … loosening up the body? Dao?'.

One must also bear in mind, even at this early hour, the city's typically warm moist air comes of lying at the juncture of the Yangtze River and the East China Sea. And of course, wherever one might be in China, there is ever present, somewhere in the distance, the ancient surrounds of a craggy mountain range. On this day, adding to the intensified atmosphere, the light rain, its tracing of minute droplets upon every little thing, even in-between things, gave everything that could be seen a glistening film. All the world looked in greater fidelity, brighter, ever more real.

The heighten reality of the clinging rain, *whispering our future*, was so intoxicating that the only objects I had thought at the time worth preserving were a teacup that Yi stole and a gaudy circus pamphlet. Later, unless my memory deceives me, a few photographs came into my possession. Our first stop was an old Naval Dockyard. The salty, fishy air lingered upon our lips as we traipsed around a large ship surrounded by junks. The novelist took photographs on a compact camera, thumbing it effortlessly between pictures to advance the film. He perched and crouched at odd angles, even rolling on the ground upon occasion. One of the guides, without translation, seemed to admonish the novelist and gestured wildly as if to suggest he was wasting his pictures. He should be taking in the grand scene, not silly little details. The novelist, equally without translation, explained he needed to fix events to things in the world, to precise geographic points and dates; suggesting these were the events his imagination 'compulsively pictured as a single vision of deliquescence'. But then, when changing the film in the back of the camera, the guide flicked the little canister out of the novelist's hands. It bounced once upon the deck before disappearing over the side, plopping satisfyingly into the sea. Leaning instinctively to see where it had ended up, we all watched as it floated there in an awakening sun, bobbing up and down in dirty froth and brine. A young dock worker in a green wicker hat and white gloves came to our aid. I looked upon the purity of his eyes and perfect oval eyebrows as he salvaged the canister from the swilling water as deftly as Yi had plucked out the little piece of cartilage with her chopsticks. As the precious load was reeled in, I had the overwhelming sense we were all at a tangent. Yet, with the film safely returned, the novelist gratefully pondered the memories within, now mixed with the silt and murk of the sea that poured out from the plastic casing. It was but one of trillions of pieces of plastic otherwise left out of sight.

By late morning we took our places in the gallery of a hospital theatre where we had been invited to attend a cataract operation under acupuncture. There was a strong smell of disinfectant. A group of doctors and nurses in white coats prepared the necessary implements and set out a series of thin, springy needles. Before the operation a small dose of sedative was applied to the patient and, on a large screen, we could see his pale face bleached by the effects of the theatre lights upon the camera lens. His eyes were open, looking tense. The doctors then began somewhat theatrically to place the needles into various pressure points upon the body. Six or seven needles were used at a time, quivering in place about the feet, arms, belly and the outer ring of the ear. The ear, we were told, has almost all the acupuncture points for the whole body.

'Why don't they put the needles in the eye?' Yi asked me, which we both agreed seemed more logical.

From where we were seated we had to fully extend our necks in order to see anything. Upon the video screen we glimpsed the stretching back of the upper eyelid, revealing the reddened perimeters of the milky white eyeball. At its centre the black marble-like pupil reflected two neat parallel lines of the fluorescent lighting above. Momentarily, with the brief glint of a scalpel, we watched the surgeon slice into the fleshy ball and saw, oozing out, a gelatinous milky fluid. Everything clouded over to a foggy moon. How strange I thought, this cut, this deliberate blindness is the means to regaining the man's sight.

Yet, by and large, the view from where we sat was mostly obscured; the pain in our necks made it difficult to sustain. In fact, all we could really see were two large feet sticking straight up from the table. The sight of the patient's big toes became strangely overwhelming. These two feet, from our angle, took on the proportions of two whole people: the big toes two big heads. Perhaps it was the disinfectant in the air, but my eyes began to widen, to take in only the view of the toes, which seemed to grow larger. I wanted to scream out, to beg others in the room if they too were seduced by these two clods of flesh. Meanwhile, Yi had grown impatient.

'I hate these eyes', she said.

I wasn't sure if she was referring to a hatred of the two big toes. Finally, however, the operation was over. The patient staggered to his feet with the uncertainty of a drunk, before then collapsing with his feet up in the air, in a dead faint.

We were taken next to a painting school. It was silent, save for the peaceful sound of brushes and inks, whereupon rows and rows of young students practised their craft. Our hosts led us through to a private room, where, shoeless, we sat cross-legged on the floor in a sweeping arch. We were offered golden tea with jasmine, served in pale blue cups with white arborescences. A long scroll was unfurled upon the floor with great pride and fastidiousness. Whispering in my ear, Yi marvelled at how the painting was not exhibited, but unfurled before us, lovingly. It's *function*, she pondered, to deepen and enhance our communion. What we saw was a magical inky world of mountains, rivers, and mist. We took a little time to adjust. It was not immediately apparent whether we were looking down upon this scene as if from afar. Or, if in fact we had been swallowed up whole by its swirling, iridescent landscape.

Yi put her hand quietly between my legs and idly played with me through my trousers while also craning to see the painting, in awe. I watched as the nape of her neck and her thin little dress blurred with the mist and streams below. We were looking at a priceless *liubai* work of the Northern Song Dynasty, so we were told. At which point, the young, rather striking looking woman in the delegation began to speak. Her cheekbones, owing perhaps something to Asian ancestry, caught the dappled light as she spoke. It was not clear if she was speaking to her hosts, to us all, or perhaps even just to herself.

'It is like *us*,' she remarked, 'there is no distinguishing among us man or women, blonde or brunette, this or that feature of face or body…'

Feigning mild frustration, the novelist seated next to me now turned his attention upon me, much to my surprise and excitement.

'Have you ever *entered* a library?', he asked. 'Not by the door', he continued, sensing perhaps that I wanted to say I had, 'but through one of the books on the highest shelf, whose title or author you cannot make out?'

Starting may be the stablest element that clusters behind the eyes, I hardly knew what to say, and strange memories were passing through my awkwardly folded legs. Perhaps sensing my uncertainty, the philosopher now leaned in.

'Don't listen to him. He wants what he wants, without the detail', and added something about the novelist's contrived weaning, more *divided than the whole milk of a poem*. At which point, in whispered tones, a playful argument broke out between them both, with each claiming to have a more radical sense of impermanence. The philosopher accused the novelist of having no footing in the picture, being eventless, and while the novelist remonstrated, the philosopher shot back something about there being a double exposure, *all* surface *and* depth. The novelist shook his head and rolled his eyes, having heard this all before. He mumbled something about fictional darkness.

'One thing neither of you seem to doubt is the importance of your own I', Yi chimed in, rather crossly.

At which point the novelist and philosopher burst out laughing. In the excitement the teapot was knocked over spilling its contents across a corner of the painting, which only made them laugh more. We did our best to distract our hosts, thinking perhaps that as it dried the tea would add its patina undetected to the prevailing mist and streams.

In hope of regaining order, our hosts ushered everyone through to the next room, yet Yi and I tarried. The room now empty, I grabbed between her legs and she seized my stiff cock that was showing through my trousers. Yi took my hand wordlessly and with our bare feet we stepped into the painting. I pulled up Yi's dress and seeing her blood-red flesh I first thrust my fingers in and then my cock. Watching as I entered that cavern of blood, she put her bony middle finger deep inside my arse. Animals can hardly fuck as hard as we did. We kissed frenetically, salvia streaming from our lips. We tumbled down like dice upon the painting, two bodies smashing into the picture from outer space. My thick penis gorged Yi's vulva as she convulsed, squirting, and everything mixed with blood from the arse. Our mucilaginous concoction flung down hard upon the painting, disfiguring the misty treetop mountains.

Thereupon the picture scattered to the four winds and, huddled together, we floated for an instance through the landscape. There was no beginning or ending. All shone through, water washing water; for all the world to see. Except, with our hearts still booming, one on top of the other, Yi now drew back into focus and I was captivated by her fragility: *a wounded tiger upon a precarious path*. There was no terror, no shame, no cuts or bites, yet the swirling mists and sparkling streams could sustain us no more and all was flat and in its place again.

Later, in the evening, we were taken to the circus where we saw all the usual splendours. The beautiful lithe bodies of the trapeze artists spun and span, entwined, almost certainly re-ordering gravity in sparkling skin-tight leotards and high-heel shoes. A majestic lion gnashed dutifully at its trainer as serene straight-backed dancers glided and looped around in a dizzying display. Later came a tightrope walker, holding a long red pole to steady himself. He was a frail looking acrobat and as he reached the midpoint of the highwire, poised delicately up in the roof of the big tent, at the far end there appeared a harlequin (*deus ex machina*).

'Get away, get away!' He hollered at the acrobat, berating him like a housefly.

And then, with a definite smirk, there being no safety net, the harlequin took hold of the wire and yanked it with tremendous force. With the shockwave that ran along its entire length *there occurred the dreadful thing that silenced every mouth and fixed every eye.* The acrobat fell to the ground in the time it takes a pebble to drop from the side of a small building. The result: a flayed, flattened body, like an ink blot.

The Ringmaster rushed to the acrobat's aid. Behind him flocked a crowd, among them the novelist with his camera. Badly injured, but not yet dead, some words were exchanged. Soon, however, the acrobat spoke no more and his hand fell from the Ringmaster, who scooped him up and carried him away, a mere cascade of robes in their arms. Whether this was planned as part of the entertainment it was not easy to tell, but all was quickly forgotten with what came next.

'Roll up, roll up!', bellowed a voice, 'gather round for tonight's grand finale: the amazing, the astounding, the inexplicable illusion of a thousand cuts!'

Down at ringside, among the paparazzi, the novelist was taking his own photographs in rapid succession. He did all he could to get the very best shot, elbowing and shoving those around him to ensure he captured the true moments of pain. Up in the stands I was transfixed by the illusion of dismemberment. Legs were crudely sawn to stumps and innards pulled between protruding rib bones. Yet the victims persisted with oddly ecstatic smiles, their accruing absences faintly erotic.

'Chronic eloquence', the Professor whimpered, with tears running down both cheeks.

Yi, however, was unimpressed, faintly bored. She

supremely, silently, rejected all the pomp. Her arse was numb from the cheap seats, and she sighed impatiently as another limb fell to the floor.

Caught up in the spectacle I had not noticed Yi was now squatting on her seat, straining at the face. It was only with the wave of a fishy, putrid smell that I turned to see what it was she was doing. Her stool come slowly down between her bare legs. She climbed out of her seat, laughing, and took hold of me. Upon the seat was her defiant dung; a steaming egg left for all to see. Like a thousand minutes in a single second, we looked hard into one another's eyes and stole away.

Rue de Richelieu

Thus, two kinds of excretions or losses, of not inconsiderable differences and consistencies, had fallen down into the world. One, the coil of steaming little shit that Yi had borne the crowd; the other, the scattered, spurting parts of bodies and their innards strewn about the circus floor. This entanglement, tied to death in ways that went far deeper than were the interests of the hungry mob, brought us back, if only momentarily, to Laura (and all that had happened between us). So vivid was this instance *I stepped forward like a sleepwalker as though about to touch her at eye level.*

Inevitably, of course, all soon went back to normal, though not without these pangs and apparitions in the immediate hours after the circus. Unusually, but borne of these circumstances, Yi entered into quite a black mood, and she told the Professor she couldn't stay any longer where we were. Instead, she wanted to see Paris, she wanted to know for herself its reputation as *la Ville-Lumière*.

Amused and inspired by Yi's impatience, the Professor took great delight in teasing her and equally satisfying the very *whims of the simplest and most angelic creature ever to walk the earth*. The next day we promptly boarded passage to Paris, where we found an altogether different intensity of light and humidity than in Shanghai. A lavish abundance of flowers in the streets, the aroma of freshly baked bread and the contrasting stench of the Metro, only helped heightened our senses. Everywhere too was graffiti, the city's great bible; an enumeration of voices, each lost one to the next. And of course, ever the sentinel, the city's great Tower gazed upon us wherever we went.

Yi walked about causally in what on close inspection would be deemed nightwear and fetish. One skirt she plucked without care from our suitcase was supposed to tie up at the back, showing the arse, but would slip round as she wandered the city, revealing her crotch through the criss-crossing of its ties.

She had taken to following people at random in short unorganised bursts, mimicking their everyday, disjointed itineraries. The Professor, who mostly lazed about drinking coffee at Café de Flore while waiting for Yi and I to return from our various forays, suggested Yi was playing *éminence grise* in other's lives.

'What do you want with these strangers?' I asked of Yi.

'Oh, nothing. No mystery, no love story', she replied.

In her present mood, it was as if she could only exist if she was on the trail of someone else, but certainly without their knowing it. If they turned around to notice her the game was lost. The only way to avoid encountering people in this great labyrinth of a city, she had said, was to follow them.

And so she went on, setting traps for others unbeknown to them. If she lost the trail for any reason she asked questions in shops and cafes in the manner of a detective. And incessantly she took photographs. Click, click, click she went. Although I'm not sure if there was ever any film loaded in the camera. She never stopped to check. On the Metro Yi *stole* many photographs. Ignoring the signs forbidding the taking of pictures, she would carefully, surreptitiously, prop the camera on her lap or balance it upon my shoulder and capture beautiful portraits of fellow passengers without their ever knowing it; all of them looking into space, all of them averting their gaze as everyone does.

'No one is looking at anyone else', she said again and again, ever amazed.

Only the camera can see what none of us look at, and so in those little moments Yi and I wondered if with each press of the shutter-release we all simply disappear.

Of course, during these excursions we never stopped having sex. Although we avoided orgasms and tried to busy ourselves with sight-seeing as this was the only means to abate ourselves. From one place to the next we could not help looking around for opportunities. An empty room at the Louvre (moments before an attendant returned), under the glow of a magnificent rose window of the cathedral, up against the Colonnes de Buren, at the back of a tour boat along the Seine, among the bushes outside the Basilique in Montmarte, overlooking a delightful, twinkling scene of the city at night, and in the numerous alleyways in and around the restaurants and cafes along the Boulevard Saint-Germain-des-Prés. All in all, we walked many miles of the city until we found the right place, and those rare instances when the bustling crowds thinned. Yi would spread herself, or I would lift one of her legs and drive inside before then disengaging as quickly as we had begun. Our genitals still throbbing with the heat, we then carried on with our aimless wanderings. On the occasions the Professor had followed us, they would generally keep their distance. And if they masturbated we would hardly know, not due to their caution, it should be said, but because theirs was a style of discretion and urbanity.

On one such occasion we were up on the Tower, which otherwise had always kept its steady watch upon us. Having dutifully taken the stairs we marvelled at all of the details: the plates, beams, and bolts, and of the fact we were inside one big model made up of segments, with all of its design laid open. Taking up the Tower's viewpoint for ourselves the three of us breathed in the city, framed in among it criss-crossing wrought iron surrounds.

'What is the point of being up here?' I asked the Professor, baffled as I was by the sheer inutility of it all.

'This is where we learn to see people as dots', they replied, smiling, 'and from those dots we gain whole new ways of living'.

Down below, encircling us was a seemingly endless parade of deadlocked traffic. The frustrated faces tucked inside the countless vehicles became, inversely, the marks of the city. Here, among the beeping horns, the stop-start of engines, and the clatter of crowds was the ricochet of all meanings.

'We are the only ones not to know our own glance', Yi mused out loud as her last coin dropped inside the unwieldy binoculars and its viewer detached like a cataract, to show only a faint blank. The Professor was at ease and mumbled under their breath, as if by rote, remarking how *the tower is the only blind point of the total optical system of which it is the centre and Paris the circumference.*

Later we found ourselves at the corner of Rue de Richelieu and Rue Colbert, whereupon the Professor stopped us in our tracks. This was a significant place we were told: the National Library.

'What is so important about that?' Yi asked.

'Go inside,' the Professor instructed, 'while we stay here. It will be good for you to walk around by yourself'.

Yi grimaced at the idea, yet nonetheless acquiesced and went inside, while I waited with the Professor, feeling deeply curious and a little envious.

Only a matter of minutes later, typical of her speed, Yi re-emerged at the entrance of the library. We were perplexed: She was almost doubling up with laughter. Indeed, she could not speak for laughter, and at the sight of which I too began to smile and soon this grew until the two of us were laughing uncontrollably. So much so we had tears streaming down our faces and we clutched at our bellies trying to remedy the pain of our cachinnations. Even the Professor could not hold back

'You daft girl!', they said, 'what are you laughing about? This is the site of great power, as decreed by Napoleon himself, the place of all the world's memories!'.

And still laughing along with us, they pointed to the brass plaque at the side of the doorway. Once one of the largest collections in the world, its origins tracing back to the fourteenth century, it survived near destruction at the time of the French Revolution, going on to become the proud property of the People. But our laughter only grew wilder and in all our amusement (still not knowing what we were laughing about) I pissed into my trousers, the darkening of cloth growing outward from my groin and trickling down to a puddle at my feet.

It was hard not to notice the effects of my accident: the outline of my shrivelled cock now discernible through the wet trousers stuck to my legs, along with the whiff of ammonia. Yi looked upon me with a smile, eyeing my little member with a hint of both mirth and lewdness.

'Not to worry, we can go into the library,' said Yi, who had recovered composure, 'you'll dry off'.

We marched into the library and immediately entered its beautiful oval reading room. While I had not been aware of the noise of the street, the cars and mopeds, the honking of horns, and the clatter of people threading passed one another, here in the reading room I was immediately aware it had all ceased. Among the occasional shifting of a chair or muffled cough from somewhere, which echoed slightly in the domed arena of the room, all was silent, save perhaps the hush of the collective breathing of the readers. High above nine ceramic clad cupolas, held upon spidery columns of iron, reflected the natural light of the huge, alien-like polished glass oculi at their centre. We were bathed in shadowless light. As we walked across the waxed wooden floor, each step clacking satisfyingly, we tried to be as quiet as we might. The Professor pulled out several draws of index cards, basking in the delight of all that was held in this cathedral of books. Yi and I spun 360 degrees marvelling at the tiered gantries all around the edge of the room, each recess lit as if little theatre stages. Then, stealing behind an enormous velvet curtain, we stepped backstage, into a large central nave surrounded by six stories of book stacks. Readers walked about its metal walkways ferrying books, searching, idling. Of course, in taking all of this in, almost without breathing, there was nothing that told of Yi's amusement.

To the contrary: this was a site of calm and inner reflection. The books surrounding us acted as sentries, so that we spoke in hushed tones and moved our bodies as in a membrane. My trousers still stuck to my groin and thighs. Yi looked upon me knowing that I was desperate to take them off and to put her upon one of the vacant desks, yet she held a finger up to halt any such thoughts. Then she silently conducted me to look the other way, pointing to an old man who stood pondering a mass of photographs set out about the floor. He stood in the middle of his haphazard grid of images, pensive and alone in one of the far corners of the reading room.

'I want to see what he sees', said Yi.

A bell rang at that very moment, and everyone was told to collect their belongings and leave. The library was closing for the evening. Yet, the old man in the far corner took no notice. He went on looking at his pictures, shuffling some of them as if ordering in some grand way. Yi and I crept closer. We waited at the corner of a desk. I could not help myself from reaching out to caress Yi's neck as we crouched together, my cock rubbing against her back. But with everyone filling out in the opposite direction and with her eyes intent on the old man, it only put her on edge and she told me to stop or she would force me to come. We lingered on, with the library now empty and still, except for this old man, who could be heard just faintly talking to himself.

'You see?' Yi said, '…he is the librarian'.

This was the key to the puzzle for which we had patiently waited. He was working intensely, oblivious to the now empty, echoing shell of the whole library. Instructing himself one way, only to then reprimand, so altering his decision yet again, he went on with his work. It was like an unfathomable game of chess; with each move he bent down to place and replace the large photographs, creating different sequences and series. There was something queer about the whole thing that I desperately held my breath to stifle the laughter now rising irrepressibly again, when the librarian suddenly came to rest: straightening his back he appeared now in full view, blue eyes, white hair, even youthful looking (incomparably to his age). In his dapper suit and with a neat looking face, he was *a very beautiful and very saintly man*.

Realising the lateness of the hour he promptly started and would most likely have vanished behind the velvet curtain if Yi, much to my surprise, had not hailed him. Something had come over her: *she greeted the visionary courteously and said she wanted to learn*. The librarian, evidently of poor sight, his eyes flitting about, and his mind no doubt still gliding through the pictures, attempted to look earnestly over in Yi's direction. He offered a brief bow and set himself down at a nearby desk without a word.

The Lesson

To watch this scene of Yi sitting down to listen to the man might have seemed innocent enough. Nevertheless, I waited, keeping my distance, feeling a general sense of unease. I could not hear what they were saying, though evidently there was nothing wrong in their manner, only I assumed the worst. I assumed there was violence in the words spoken, which would mark upon our most impious girl. At any moment I told myself I should be ready to break things up, yet still on the face of it nothing happened. The librarian took out paper and pen and seeming to anticipate the very words before they formed, Yi nodded agreements and murmured affirmations. The man wrote with a slow and methodical hand precipitating only small spidery lines. Upon making any little errors he earnestly overwrote with redactions of neat cross-hatchings, going back and forth, diagonally left and right. Yi gave the impression of learning a great deal, whereas in fact it was hard to know who was leading who in this little dance. They remained in dialogue in this way for some time, Yi occasionally voicing aloud some of what the librarian was jotting down, and that was all.

I was exchanging glances with the Professor standing by my side, both of us hinting at something, yet not quite manifesting as to anything certain, when in front of us things now became apparent. Yi was consoling the old man. She ran her hand over his frail legs, softly caressing him, only she could not feel his cock, which led her to smile. The librarian, his eyes rolling upward as blind men's do, let out a little laugh to make light of the situation, yet he knew his time had come.

I had moved closer now, standing by Yi's side in hope of seeing properly what was to happen: Yi was undoing the librarian's buttons, she had lowered herself to his knees, and at last she found his cock. It was shrivelled and flaccid just like the flap of skin from the top of the cockerel. She pumped it gently with two hands. I distinctly heard her say:

'Father, you can name all your pictures for me, but do you know what I see?'

A few seconds of silence.

'The worst of it is, if I tell you, you'll say I am only telling you what you already know…'

More seconds went by, his penis flapping helplessly in her clasp.

'If you don't believe me, I can show you', she added.

At which point Yi stood up and dragged the old man to his pictures, which remained in their neat rows across the floor. There were pictures of copulating figures and phalluses of the Aurignacian period, big busted ivory statues, Corinthian dancers, many Satyrs, raw, erect fauns, visions of hell, fondling couples, Lucretius taking a dagger, quartered bodies, the head of Holofernes served on a platter, Death caressing nudes, nymphs fucking from behind, hermaphrodites, a weeping Venus, a worn-out Oedipus, haggard Tiresias and a distracted Narcissus, Medusa's head with eyes of terror, the horrors of war, Mary Magdalen, three witches, a gloating imp, matrimonial madness, flagellators, cannibals, the chateau of the Marquis de Sade, a woman in stockings, a thick, dark etching of Olympia, orgies at La Maison Tellier, a Van Gogh nude, masked women, a praying mantis, a lunar city, reclining, spent figures, a dwarf between splayed, voluptuous thighs, voodoo sacrifices (tarred and feathered), bombed-out trucks of an Iraqi supply line, and finally those scenes from the circus - if I was not mistaken, the very same photographs taken by the novelist.

'Mr Librarian,' Yi cried out theatrically, jabbing her fingers at the various photographs, 'you can toss yourself off.'

And she yelled some more, telling him to look as if looking for her; commanding him to bend over, to look back at her through his legs. The librarian duly did as he was told, or at least bent as far as he could, which wasn't nearly far enough. Cross and impatient Yi now darted her foot in an unflinching strike, kicking away the backs of the old man's spindly legs. He immediately fell, dead weight, too winded to make a sound, only his sagging body letting out a wheeze. His fly was open, his cock dangling, his face flushed. He didn't resist; his breathing was laboured.

'My friends,' the librarian gasped, 'I myself am old'.

'At least you had the right to look', the Professor retorted.

'Through the *whites* of your eyes', I added.

'Yes, it is alright for you Old Man!', said Yi.

All this while, the Professor looked upon us inscrutably as ever, but also had taken to looking about further, surveying the scene. They soon fixed upon the ornate spiral staircase that led to the mezzanine where row upon row of books glowed in the recesses of golden lamp light.

'Show us your books, teach us something we don't already know!'

We hauled the suffering man to his feet and like puppeteers each took an arm or a leg to help him wind his way up the stairs. He groped his way along the shelves, feeling here and there, giving a running commentary of a certain history of knowledge. Following behind we pulled these various highlights from the shelves and proceeded to disabuse the old man of his stories. Some beautifully bound, others tatty and torn, some large in format, others neat like prayer books, we yanked the various volumes from the shelves and played with them. One old book, a certain Chinese encyclopaedia, presented all kinds of taxonomies and wild illustrations, including pictures of animals that from a long way off looked like flies. The Professor fell about laughing.

'All the familiar landmarks of *our* thought! All the ordered surfaces and all the planes with which we are accustomed to tame!'

Picking up books at random we spat into their bindings so our saliva dribbled through to the floor, we stacked several volumes end to end and attempted to piss over the top of them, and we wanked across double-spreads and promptly slammed the books shut, listening to the pages sigh. Out of one volume (a thick, squat book, bound in gold) fluttered a picture postcard. Seemingly a long-lost bookmark, I picked it up and found immediately that it was, how to put it, obscene.

A little man stood behind a seated scribe. He was prodding at the scribe's shoulder with a bony finger, his other hand wagging angrily, as if dictating at pace. But his robe was ruched up and without doubt he was sodomising the scribe, whose bent leg, appearing awkwardly out from where he was seated betwixt a cramped desk and chair, might have been mistaken for the impatient man's thrusting shaft, as if penetrating right through the scribe; this *insane hubris of his prick, an interminable, disproportionate erection.* I spun the card around to show Yi, thrusting it before her eyes.

'Imagine the day, when we will be able to send sperm by post card', she laughed.

At which point, Yi pulled the librarian back from his meanderings, from his groping about the shelves. She pushed him face-first into the books nearest to us, their spines blurring in our proximity. She swiped the postcard sharp across his cheek, a fine line of blood, a paper cut, appeared in micro-droplets, and she vigorously played with herself all the while whispering and licking in the librarian's ear. Overcome with these exaltations I fucked Yi in the arse. The books, now all pushed to the back of the shelf, a faint hollow of our ménage à trois.

'Enough delay,' the Professor called out, 'enough of your deferments!'. The Professor had grown weary and complained that these books were only everything we already knew.

'Where are those you keep under lock and key?' they asked.

The librarian could not help but give the game away, instinctively, if furtively, glancing towards a nondescript cabinet. We rifled through the contents, whereupon the Professor pulled out a stack of files, each held in fonds, which they held aloft gloriously like a trophy. The files were marked with the letters of the alphabet, diligently wrapped and ordered. Like a pack of hungry animals we pulled out the various papers, quickly mixing them up despite the protestations of the librarian.

'Look,' the Professor explained, 'these are the most coveted papers, yet they are nothing more than the work of a copy clerk gone mad; farcical notes on iron, glass, façades, prostitutes, cafés and advertisements: *art enters the service of the merchant!*'

'These papers smell like come', Yi said.

'No surprise,' the Professor continued, 'a hotchpotch of citations, the lost time in the spaces of things, these are the *actual* precipitations of hundreds of years of blood, sweat and come. Yet, as much as we might foretell these worlds, ours is a *resolute effort to distance ourselves from all that is antiquated.* And these pathetic notes are nothing but fossils!'

Yi and I had indeed wondered what was so precious and the lucidity of the Professor's remarks now gave us no further need for explanation. There was nothing here that had not been written before. Convinced as we were, it seemed only fitting to put their archival value to the test.

'Let's burn the papers!' Yi cried (her desire to set fire to things still unquenched, I suspect, from that time we left the moped to rust upon the beach).

The librarian was by now experiencing severe palpitations, holding his chest, and still protesting between hard gasps for air. The Professor threw several of the files into the wastepaper bin and struck a match.

'Maybe through the flames we will see a treasure map!'

We watched for a while in silence as the dry papers frittered away in the curling flames. The Professor continued to add files so that the heat built up in the room.

'It is sweltering in here!' Yi said in a voice that could have come from each of us. 'Now it's time to piss', she added, speaking directly to the librarian.

For sure enough, if the flames were not soon doused the risk was of a fire ripping through the many centuries of the library. The old man did as instructed. And with his penis turgid from pissing, Yi took the opportunity to masturbate the librarian, his come finally flopping into the mass of charred and still smouldering papers.

Legs of a Phage

With the last drop of urine and come having dribbled from his cock, the librarian staggered backwards losing his footing. We tried to catch him, only we became muddled in our efforts and he crashed to the floor.

The Professor, Yi, and I stood still, gazing down, each thinking how small this old man now seemed; his feet disproportionate to his thin legs, his gaunt neck betraying his true age despite the sparkle of his baby blue eyes. We smiled as he lay there with a limp cock, still done up in his neat, tailored suit, his pocket-watch still securely fastened by its chain to his waistcoat. Now that his balls were drained he appeared sanguine, though he held both hands tightly to his chest. We sensed the air escaping as from a punctured tire as he sighed.

'I never did set sail with a boat full of migrants…', he

muttered, along with other incomprehensible remarks.

The Professor gave Yi and me a little nod and we promptly set to work to lift the old man, though we soon got the giggles and it took us many attempts.

'Get on your feet,' the Professor ordered the librarian, 'you're going to fuck one of us…'

'Consider it my gift, my sacrifice…', the librarian replied graciously, though sounding mildly inebriated, and his voice fast fading with the shortness of breath.

'You are forgetting you have trashed this library. Your forensics are all over it.'

The librarian recovered a little at this point. He remained placid, even serene. A gentle smile came over him: 'I have sat among these same books day after day. I have sat here at the edges of the world, while you my voyeur, what have you done?'

'You fool', snapped the Professor, '*Voyeur*? Do you think I am going to let you trick us into believing the mere signs, the sheer debris of your supposed absorption? None of this shit and spit matters, no more than your own shit and spit.'

'Yes, you can imitate everyone you know,' softly sang the librarian, 'I told you so. All… you want… is *you*…'

'Let us re-tell your story', said the Professor with renewed, steely calm.

'You well know, my friend, that men like you have such stiff cocks the moment their respiration is cut; that they ejaculate. Let us give you that last rite. We owe you that much. Let us bear witness to your final excretions.'

What followed next I can only really describe as an operation. From behind, the Professor thrust their arms out straight under the armpits of the old man. A mere scarecrow, his arms splayed, his feet dragging, the librarian tremoring from his own lack of breath. I undid his belt from his waist, which we then wrapped several times around his neck, pulling tighter and tighter.

'So now,' the Professor said to us both, '*know* this father of yours…'

The librarian's trousers had fallen to the floor without the belt. Yi removed her dress, and with the grace of a ballet dancer knelt and took the old man's cock in her mouth. My own cock was thick and hard. I took it out and from behind I thrust myself deep into the librarian.

'Now', continued the Professor, 'take the belt, both of you, pull it hard, imagine how it squeezes on the pipe just behind the Adam's apple'.

We did as commanded. As much as I was forcing myself inside, I also pulled as hard as I might on one end of the belt. Yi took the other. We felt a dreadful shudder as we gradually garrotted the man. His cock now stood on end. Yi jumped up, wrapping her legs around both the librarian and me. We continued to squeeze the throat as we both fucked him hard.

Utterly intoxicated by the pulsating of two hard cocks, my own inside the man, and his inside Yi, our muscles clenched with deepening pain, while those of the librarian soon faded away. Whether it was the force of our pulling on the belt, or simply the old man's cardiac arrest, Yi felt his warm come shooting inside her. She reeled from his clutches, shaking with joy.

Yi lay upon the floor of the library. Her thighs were smeared with her own sweat and the dead man's sperm, which had leaked out from inside her as soon as she had pulled herself away. I lay down next to her. I wanted so much to now mount her and fuck her in turn, yet all I could bring myself to do was hold her in my arms and kiss her.

'We are an entity,' I whispered.

'…so, here for infinity', she replied, with a sweet smile.

For some moments we lay in a gentle paralysis caused by the certain sense of love for one another and the spasms of death of the man beside us, whose life (despite the wide-open stare of his glassy eyes) was now erased like those faces seen drawn with a stick in the sand at the edge of the sea. I have never been so content.

At last Yi sat up. And disentangling herself from me, she moved across to look directly at what we had done. She squatted over the half-naked cadaver and looked intently at its ashen face. She stroked a cheek and then held the head in two hands. From the library's large domed ceiling came the soft red hue of the now sinking sun, which glanced across the dead face. Yi gave a small shiver, and something lit up inside her. Leaning in close to the body and with delicate fingers, she pulled back the lid of one eye to peer deep inside. Her inspection took some time. She squinted to see as minutely as she might, though likely was only able to see the fading rivers of arteries. Sitting back up she took the dead man's hands into her own and appeared to offer a brief prayer and reflection.

Curiously enough, we were not worried about what needed to happen. The library was closed to the public and while perhaps some cleaners might possibly have come along, the Professor and I would have soon ushered them away. Yi slowly revived from her meditations and we drew together to survey the scene. We agreed it expedient to move the body, if only to give ourselves time. As it turned out, we need not have bothered. The old librarian had not urinated nearly enough. Unbeknown to us, as we busied ourselves with the body, the embers in the wastepaper bin had reignited, fuelled further by the bundles of files. To cut a convoluted story short, the library burnt to the ground. Of course, this was to come later. As it was, we dragged the corpse passed the velvet curtain, along the metal walkways between thousands of books. Despite being now away from the glare of the reading room, the criss-crossing viewpoints of the six storied stack gave little or no cover. We hauled the dead man to the far end where we came to a conservation laboratory. By now we were perspiring from our load and we drew a breath as the Professor picked the lock. In a final effort we then bundled the body inside.

We had entered a white, sterilised room. There were shimmering stainless steel counters and an array of implements, machines, and chemical preparations. Taking it all in, the Professor remarked how such things might be *useful*. Yi could think of nothing more horrifying.

'Professor', she said, rubbing her cheek gently on their shoulder, 'I want you to do something'.

'I shall do anything you like,' they replied.

Yi brought us back to the corpse. She knelt and opened an eye.

'Do you see it?' She asked.

'Well?'

'I want to see what this sees', she said plainly.

'Look here,' I urged her, extremely disturbed, 'what are you getting at?'

'I want to play with this eye. I want to know all that it has seen, and what more it still sees.'

'What do you mean?'

'Professor,' she pleaded, 'you must give me this *egg* at once, tear it out, I want it!'

The Professor was never one to show emotion, except perhaps when embarrassed, when there was no physiological way to hide it. Now, without seeming to bat an eyelid, the blood nonetheless swelled upon their face. They picked up a pair of sturdy scissors from a nearby bench, knelt down, then nimbly eased back one of the sockets, drew out the eyeball with one hand, while with the other cut firmly at the stubborn ligaments. Before presenting the small bloody eyeball to Yi, the Professor held it thoughtfully between finger and thumb. And, in looking about the laboratory, the need was clear. Against the far wall was some large complicated looking machinery which nestled around a central column.

'An electron-microscope. Now, my girl, you will see what you want to see...'

The Professor placed the eyeball between a pair of tweezers and explained how we would need to coat it in a fine layer of gold. We watched avidly as they performed the task and soon enough before us glimmered a little matt gold bauble. They placed it into a small chamber and started up the microscope.

A monitor flickered into life and as the machine warmed up, we began to see a cloudy image appear. The Professor pressed various buttons and spun a central controller. Soon a 'picture' came into view.

'We are looking deep inside the eye,' the Professor declared.

'There's an alien!' Yi cried out, recoiling from what she saw, cowering half behind me.

Sure enough, through the murky image now appeared, quite distinctly, a small creature. It appeared to look straight at us.

'A phage!' The Prorfessor explained.

'It has long legs, like an alien invader,' Yi spoke, biting her lips. She and I couldn't help but think it might step out of the machine at any moment and train its single beady eye upon us from atop its spidery limbs.

'It's harmless', the Professor laughed. But so as to reassure us, they began playing with the controller again and the phage disappeared.

'Now we are far far inside. We are seeing thousands of nanometres inside the eye…'

But all we could see was what looked like a marvellous night sky. We were looking down the wrong end of a telescope: a view of deep, deep space, where everything stretched out further and further apart and in-between was all inky black.

It is hard to say how long we gazed into the absurdity of this realm. What appeared both a void and an engulfing whole *all at the same time*, slowly grew upon us as our eyes adjusted to the great expanse. It was Yi who eventually pulled us from our slumber. She could take it no longer and reached inside the small chamber to reclaim *her* eye. She instantly amused herself by toying with it between her thighs. The gold leaf yellowed her skin before she inserted it between her legs and pulled it out again, its golden hue now glazed with her own fluids. After repeating this a few times the painted surface was gradually washed away to reveal once more the small whitish eyeball beneath.

'The caress of the eye,' Yi told us, 'is so utterly, so extraordinarily gentle; so bizarre that it has something of a rooster's nasty crowing'.

Much to my surprise, Yi now put the eye straight in her mouth and rolled it around several times, savouring it, caressing it with her tongue. She drew it out upon her lips, looking as if she were now kissing it, and in that instance, as the eye stared out at the Professor and me, Yi appeared to have a face with three eyes. Then, all of a sudden, she spat it out like a cherry stone. The eye dropped noisily upon the belly of the corpse, an inch or so from the cock.

By this time, the Professor was helping me out of my clothes so I could offer myself naked to the 'girl who had just spat out an eye'. The entire length of my cock slid effortlessly into Yi's hairy vagina. We fucked joyously as the Professor picked up the eyeball and rolled it precariously about our writhing bodies, across the skin of our chests and down our backs.

'Let me trap it between your navels', the Professor urged.

'No, put it up my arse,' shouted Yi in reply.

The Professor guided the eye down Yi's back, down between her buttocks. But Yi now grabbed it out of the Professor's hands and with one deft action it disappeared through her hair between her legs with a satisfying sucking sound. She pulled me close and suckered her lips to mine with such force I came instantly, my come shot across her pubic hair.

As I stood up from our heap of bodies, Yi eased her legs apart and I found myself face to face with what I imagine I had always already expected, yet still it cut like a wire. Staring straight between Yi's thighs, nested inside her, I saw the wan blue eye of *Laura* gazing back at me through tears of urine. The come still steaming through the hair gave that vision an oneiric, film-like quality, a melancholic air. Yi gave off a spasm, her burning urine streamed out from under the eye down to the floor...

Only hours later we were sauntering through the streets of Paris wearing ridiculous outfits so as to disguise ourselves. The Professor admiringly described Yi as bedizened in an oversized hat with flowers; that she looked for all the world to be a noble girl from the provinces. We procured a huge valise and packed it with all number of pilfered garments, make-up and wigs. With these preparations complete we stole a car and took a long journey, making only brief stops so as not to draw attention to ourselves and to outwit any ensuing police investigation. We made our way down through Tours, skirted around Bordeaux, and kept to the coast, away from the foothills of the Pyrenees. Perhaps against our better judgement we tarried somewhat in Bilbao. It was there we caught a glimpse of the news, when we first heard that the library had burnt to the ground. A reporter glibly remarked how all that now remained was what had been scanned and stored upon massive server farms; that it was only a fraction of what had been lost.

We kept disappearing as best we could through the various city suburbs and along interconnecting trunk roads. Eventually, passing through Salamanca and down through Merida we arrived days later into Seville. The streets were overrun with a carnival atmosphere. We had arrived at the very height of the festival of Sanfermines. There was nothing for it but to abandon the car. We slipped into the anonymity of an enthralled crowd as they chased the bull runners ever onward. We knew our time was borrowed and we would each need go our separate ways.

Indeed, I remember it all too vividly. I looked away for one moment, but which now feels like an eternity. My gaze had turned to the sight of a desolate man (or woman?) sat crumpled at a large interchange; the sulphur of the stalled traffic their furthest concern. Dishevelled, stuck upon the central reservation with a bucket of coins, they were not blind, but instead held out a look of utter nothingness. When I next looked around, I realised both the Professor and Yi had disappeared.

I later heard the Professor had taken up residence with a

dubious billionaire. Had I cared to look, they could be found sailing a yacht in some out of the way jurisdiction. I know nothing of where Yi stole away. We always knew it almost impossible to find a cure for love. I have only a single postcard. It shows a picture of a beautiful witch looking around corners. I rarely bring myself to turn it over, to see her neat handwriting to *my love*:

'Our image, our reflection was never ours alone. Can we live in such a way love emerges in the in-between? Don't let anything suggest there is no us. *I would like to write you so simply, so simply, without having anything ever catch the eye, excepting yours alone…*'

A quarter of a century on, I live out my days modestly amid the mild climes of the southern coast of the Iberian Peninsula.

2. PREPARATION

It is often said there are no such things as coincidences. And indeed the composing of this partly imaginary tale would never have been possible without various incidents and intersections. Since they are woven through the 'meaning' of what I have written, I would like to describe them.

Of course, there is always a dilemma in presenting a commentary *upon* a text. Not just for the obvious reasons in the case of fiction of unseating a suspension of disbelief. More than that, there is, as Roland Barthes observes, 'a *rivalry* between the world and the work'. Kafka is a prime example: 'he always experienced the world as something hostile to literature, that made him suffer, sometimes to the point of panic'. Any attempt here to offer an 'understanding' of the Text would surely be folly, and equally the temptation is to look at things from the other direction, to suggest that literature (the Work) might be a therapeutic offered in reply to the world. The remarks noted here from Barthes are taken from his lecture course on the preparation of the novel. While there is not much one can actually learn from this course in terms of 'how to' write a novel, what is explored is the existential act of writing. In writing the 'work', he suggests, the attempt is to exhaust a 'space', which in reality is inexhaustible. In doing so we come to meet ourselves in ways that are not always expected. The tendency is for writing to lead to disappointment, but this is largely due to how we mythologise ourselves; suggesting to ourselves that we are *more* than what we write. But what if we are less than we think we are, and that it is in fact through writing that we can become more? What follows here is hardly biography (and only a partial bibliography), because even if I could conceive of such an account, what accrues in the Text is only one reading, or 'way' through; a cutting across of an inter-text: only ever, then, a *preparation*. As Barthes puts it at the very start of his course: 'better the illusions of subjectivity than the impostures of objectivity. Better the Imaginary of the Subject than its censorship'.

I began the writing during confinement, the result of a major pandemic. Inevitably, it was a time that prompted many to reflect on a much deeper sense of enclosure; the general sense of having forgotten all desires. In truth, I had begun making mental notes many years before, yet it was during this period of isolation that I finally committed to the *form* that the work could properly take. However, if I were to set a specific date for its origins I would go back further to a particular incident as a junior lecturer at X, shortly after the millennium. To this day I can replay in my head a seminar during which a rather obnoxious male student said something that stopped me in my tracks.

I forget his actual name, though I still recall his face: Blonde and pale, with a longish face and piercing eyes. He gave off a permanent smirk, that of a cocky troublemaker, the kind who harbours his own deep insecurities. A smirk nonetheless that haunted me week in, week out. In lieu of his actual name we can imagine a good white, middle-class one, since, all things considered, despite my own hard to see ambiguities (which I shall not go into here), I will let this stand a simple *tête-à-tête*. The class had been asked to rank various phenomena in terms of 'high' and 'low' culture; a typical exercise to get everyone talking. When coming to discuss a particular female pop star (then at the height of her fame), and who it was noted was perhaps not treated with sufficient respect due to her sex, there was an occasion to introduce the feminist critique of the 'gaze'. It was at this point the student simply blurted it out:

'She *is* sexy. That's all there is to it. She is just really sexy — we don't need all this *theory*'.

On one level, his remark simply performed the problem of the gaze to perfection. Yet equally, more troublingly, his position left no room for exchange. There was no room for negotiation. This was the position of a terrorist and it happened in front of everyone. My cover was blown (and there is no way back once you have exhibited fear). Years later, I considered perhaps he might have been 'right', that the problem persists as there is no competing theory of the gaze (aside perhaps Allen Jones' forniphilia, but that is fraught with problems and only allusory). The gaze, it would seem, is equally without exchange. Back then, however, this was the least of my concerns. For the remainder of the term, I was confronted with the student's persistent, nasty grin. Underneath his expensive tracksuit I always sensed his virile adolescence. Every class there it was: his long face, with its grimaces and smirks. His head was like that of a horse protruding above everyone else. And so the days rolled on. Each week I braced myself. He pushed me. He provoked. I responded by making my class *more* explicit, although, after all these years, I forget the details.

There is a pornography, a perversity of the male gaze in that it forces the look. It forces an individual to realise and look in a certain way, even though you were going to do so anyway. And this is what is particular and peculiar about pornography: it is a way of *looking at looking* that requires no critical distance, or rather it binds such distance within itself. Of course, it is also the construction of *pleasure* that, if anything, deadens pleasure; it makes pleasure two dimensional, and so out of reach. Susan Sontag, in her essay 'The Pornographic Imagination', delineates three different pornographies: as social history, as psychological phenomenon (symptomatic of deficiencies, deformities and consumptions), and also as art. It is this sort of intellectualising that might equally prompt smirks and indignations. Surely, *pornography is pornography is pornography*. The pornographic 'look' telescopes us in and out of a scene: you are no longer just fucking, you are fucking in a role; you are in a system of fucking. You can take the pleasure it affords, but it becomes a choice, a selection and so is *finite*. Hence the observation that the art of pornography is ultimately about death, not sex.

Worse than death, we tend to forget the male gaze (the actual experience of it) is rather dull. By contrast I am inclined to think of Jenny Saville's paintings. Not the ones everyone knows, which simply turn the gaze upside down (with the neat contour lines scratched into gigantic figures evoking a geography, a system of coordinates). I'm thinking of her later works where we find bodies *together*, such as an infant wrestling in a mother's arms, couples embracing, a fight, and children playing in the sand. These portraits echo Henri Michaux's suggestion of 'a drawing as it were desiring to withdraw into itself'. These are the wild landscapes one can truly become lost in. The *art* of pornography, then, is not simply a concern for the physical act of looking, but a massive 'archive' of *possibles*, of implied, half-remembered instances of looking. We need to remember to *keep looking* rather than avert our gaze. Saville's paintings ask more about what we share in our looking than what we expose. They also leave us wondering, back in our own lives, if anyone is even there for the exchange.

My angst over the classroom scene might seem misplaced, hyperbolic even. However, there is a kink in the tale. Several years before taking up my lectureship I had in fact worked in the music industry and what is more I was acquainted with the very same pop star we had discussed so explicitly. I never let this fact be known, but inevitably it was on my mind. For a certain period of my life I knew first-hand the supposed 'allure' of this woman, who appears as K. in the Text. On numerous occasions, when frequenting studios and rehearsal rooms, I drew K., making quick sketches before she would move (she never kept still). I only ever looked at her, never upon the paper. I liked how I could travel the length of her body like a river, rather than snap it up like a crocodile. It has been said drawing is like an eye-graft, 'a grafting of one point of view on another'. All marks are displaced (even those of the camera). During those times she taught me how drawing caresses as much as inscribes. Unlike the words I use here to describe her, drawing has no need to trust in the memory of signs. Nevertheless, my drawings are all lost today. What remains, strangely enough, is a rather prosaic sense of guilt (far removed from the guilt of a pornography).

Soon after having met K. I indirectly caused her much ire (though she never knew I was involved, and it is unlikely an episode she would even now recollect). The company I worked for had numerous illustrious, high-profile clients. Discretion was paramount. In lead up to a television appearance the production team asked for a cassette recording of K.'s then unreleased album. This was common practice as such a recording was not of 'broadcast quality' and so would not break an embargo. I was tasked to prepare the cassette and duly sent it off to the studio. However, that evening, the TV presenter (known for his unpredictable antics) conjured a cassette player in the middle of the interview and live on air played snippets of K.'s new songs. The next day my boss was locked away in his office for several hours pleading with K.'s management for her to stay on as a client.

Throughout those days I can honestly say I was never really starstruck, but of everyone K. was my favourite and deep down I always felt I let her down. It is, of course, a trivial incident, but perhaps the guilt grafted upon another incident, as in the ensuing days the news broke that Princess Diana (allegedly the most photographed woman in history) died tragically in a car crash. K.'s new album was immediately held back for fear it would seem in poor taste and ultimately it was never released. The moment was lost and so ensued a definite lull in K.'s career.

The writing of fiction allows a return of many things we hardly know of or have no intention of exploring. In Nietzsche's sense, we become what we are when we write. Numerous other incidents weave their way through the Text. One small example can be given to the reference of setting light to a moped. This was a truly bizarre consideration as I wrote it, except when this image returned at the end of the story (characterised as a repressed urge; a wish to burn the evidence no less) it occurred to me this was indeed a long-suppressed memory. Staying over at a friend's house, with his parents away for several days, my friend and I met up with another school friend (who I knew less well) and we took to wandering the streets in the early hours. It was then that we stole a gleaming new motorbike parked up in front of a nearby house. We had no intention of riding it, besides there was no way of starting up the engine. We simply wheeled it off as a sacrifice. What followed was the unspeakable, clockwork-like behaviour of a pack of juveniles. Years later, I came to learn my two companions had likely been high, which left me wondering if I had been the only one to have *witnessed* the incident, and by extension to be the more culpable. I wonder too what it means to carry these 'images' when no one else can. This is a side of the gaze we seldom broach.

Of course, I have not really explained *why* the Text takes the form that it does. Upon reflection I am inclined to say two astonishing pictures lie somewhere at the heart of things. They are both pictures of the human form, the female body to be precise, and both present me with a singular anxiety. It is not an anxiety of gender, or sex, or otherness. It is rather bleaker than that. It is an anxiety about the death *always still to come* and the love that always prefigures yet is revealed only ever after the fact. The first of these pictures is a painting by my father that hung in the family home throughout my childhood.

As a child the picture unnerved me. Painted with very fine lines, it depicts a spindly figure of a young woman who is skipping. In the distance a faint horizon line gives the feeling of great expanse. The throw of the rope and the figure of the body cast a definite, yet enigmatic shadow, which is not quite in keeping with the women's actual form. Her outstretched arms and the throw of the rope that reach out from the dark shadow of her body project an image of a claw-like appendage which holds in its grasp a large egg. Sometimes before going to bed, I would shudder before the picture and not want to go up in the dark. My father would laugh gently when I said there was a strange egg in the picture. He would try to reassure me, telling me it was a happy picture of a young woman skipping. As I grew older and the effects of the picture waned, I would still dispute the image of the women skipping, saying it was of an egg. Equally, it seemed, my father only saw it his way too.

To listen to him, my father could often be mistaken for a philistine. He would openly say he saw no point in 'modern' art and through my schooling he would tactfully (for he was never one to impose) steer me away from anything lacking utility. Perhaps I would become a lawyer or doctor (later, as the world changed, the computer engineer entered the repertoire). Besides, he would say, you can always enjoy art without needing to *pursue* it. In this way my father instilled in me the importance of what is *feasible*. Yet, despite this, there *it* was: his enigmatic painting forever hanging in the house, a totem. If nothing else, what pleases us in painting is the obligation to look.

As I later came to learn, the painting is a painstaking copy of a small work by Salvador Dali, part of his *Alice and Wonderland* series from 1969. My father had spotted it featured on the front of a newspaper supplement (heralding the release of a limited-edition book, far out of anyone's reach). Dali's image is a simple pen sketch (and acts as a frontispiece, quite different to a colourful series of heliogravure prints that accompany the actual *Alice* text). In scaling up the picture, my father copied Dali line by line, but with watercolours and ink; the line of each brush mark remarkably like that of a pencil. His craftsmanship is testament to an excess of patience (despite having two young children at the time and living in a Britain that was then even more horribly divided and exclusionary).

On first reading *Story of the Eye*, I never really understood the play of the metaphor with eggs, the apparently 'ancient and closely associated obsessions, *eggs* and *eyes*', and even less so Simone's own obsession. And yet this coincidence: the Dali egg that held over me throughout the time I was growing up. The painting is held in a large, unadorned metal frame about a metre high and inset within a grey border. Everything about it is modest, yet clear. At some point, perhaps during a period of redecoration, the glass of the frame cracked. The years rolled by without anyone getting around to fix it. To this day above the arch of the skipping rope is another line from a single long crack in the glass. Beneath that line will be the mark of the years, the recording of the natural ageing process and a long scar of tobacco from my father's incessant smoking. The longer the passage of time the more indelible the mark will have become. It is surely now a deep part of the structure of the painting, so much so I fear to open it. Indeed, I associate this mark with my life-long fear that my father's smoking will be the death of him. Even writing this leads me to fear a certain equilibrium has been disturbed. Like Marcel Duchamp's *Large Glass,* I prefer to think of the 'Dali' painting as 'definitively unfinished'. In turn, this brings me to the second picture.

The purloined copy of *Story of the Eye* that I have long held in my possession has for its cover image an artwork by Duchamp. This is the other astonishing picture: a study for

Etant donnés: 1. la chute d'eaule, 2. gaz d'éclairage (c.1946-8). It is hard to know if it is an image of beauty or horror, or indeed some formulation of both at the same time. The ability for images to be simultaneously multiple underlies much of what Barthes no doubt means by exhausting a space that in 'reality' is inexhaustible. The picture in this case is a preparatory piece for Duchamp's strange final work, *Étant donnés* (1946-1966), which he developed in secret over the last two decades of his life. As is well-documented, in 1923, having abandoned *The Large Glass*, Duchamp declared an end to making art, preferring instead to devote himself to chess.

The discovery that he had in fact long been toiling with a work at the end of his life came as a shock (embarrassment?) to the art world. The work in question is a complex installation, all housed behind a large wooden door. The visitor enters a room that is empty apart from the wooden door, which is built into one of the surrounding walls. All one can do is peer through some of the slates and cracks, revealing behind, at some distance, the life-like torso of a woman, her face obscured. Like the preparatory work that appears on the cover of *Story of the Eye*, the skin of the torso for the installation is made of parchment, which gives the figure a subtle translucence that is disarming. Perhaps only Cindy Sherman's use of prostheses and masks comes close, yet these works are arguably too polished.

With *Étant donnés* it is possible you have arrived at a murder scene. A savage murder (given the state of the figure, the cleft between her legs). Yet bizarrely one arm of the figure protrudes to hold up a burning gas lamp. Classified a 'sculpture' by the Cassandra Foundation, and with a long list of building materials, organic and inorganic, as its 'medium', the work has attracted a huge amount of scholarship, the sort of painstaking efforts a virile student might abhor. When pouring over the obsessive cataloguing of every little piece and prototype related to the installation, including bronze casts (of copper-electroplated plaster originals) of the negative space of the figure's genitals (*Feuille de vigne femelle*, 1950), you can't help but think Duchamp always intended to have the last laugh.

But the installation seems overly clumsy to me. Instead, returning to the preparatory study that appears on the cover of *Story of the Eye*, I have long been haunted by its *irrealism*, its unpredictability. I can account for Duchamp's figure as figure (the figure of a woman no less), and yet there is no physics I know of that accounts for the ability to appear both alive and dead, serene and mutilated at the same time. For many years I wrapped the cover in plain paper to keep it from the prying eyes of a young child. If you had asked me why exactly I felt the need to do so I would have failed to answer. It is not that there is anything calculable and definable about this image. No, it is indeed its very unpredictability that I papered over. When I see this figure I am lost for words. I see it first one way, then another, and back to the other and so it goes on. For thousands of years civilisations have been caught up in illusions, not least centuries of religious fantasies (filled to the brim with images and their discontents). But what comes after when these fantasies have failed? This is where the story of the eye takes hold, *étant donnés*...

Of course, in composing this partly imaginary story I was making a deliberate choice to re-read and re-write Bataille's *Story of the Eye*. It has been said that to write *on* Bataille is only to betray him. The point being, that to make any kind of sense or order out of Bataille, to write in an expository sense *about* Bataille, is only to negate his *practice* of heterology. We would do well to remember how Julia Kristeva, in her essay

'Bataille, Experience and Practice', is clear *not* to make a distinction between the theoretical and erotic texts. It is Bataille's 'sovereign subject', she writes, that refuses 'all positions, all fixations', and who then can show the way towards the possibility of a 'new subject' and so the potential of an '*other* society'.

What then if one chooses instead to write like or with Bataille? Most likely the outcome is simply one of failure; the preceding story is at the mercy of the reader in this respect. But at least failure is not to betray. And however much I may have doubted the writing (and still do), there was nonetheless a point when it all seemed to get beyond me. To borrow Bataille's words (on the writing of his novel), there came a point when I was 'as happy as ever', experiencing a kind of 'fulminating joy'. Indeed, there came a point, a tipping point, when I just knew the project had to be taken to its inevitable conclusion, when I realised (when it became a compulsion) that 'nothing can wipe it away'. And importantly, as Bataille puts it: 'Such joy, bordering on naive folly, will forever remain beyond terror, for terror reveals its meaning'. And if I had given up halfway through, as was nearly the case, I was pulled back into the writing after hearing a recording of Nina Power. A somewhat waspish performance, she reminds of the pertinence *now* in re-reading Bataille; of the need to ask questions that are otherwise obscured by our modern, hygienic, utilitarian and homogeneous ways of living.

I cannot of course claim to show the possibility of a new subject, not least as the sad fact soon emerges there is no way *today* to write like Bataille. There is no *other* society. To write 'like' Bataille is likely only the conservative act to place everything in quote marks. Yet, this outcome was pre-destined.

Bored with school I abruptly left in favour of completing my general education at a run-down college. Shorn of uniform and petty rituals I was at ease, alert to new possibilities. It was here I met two hourly paid teachers, J.L. and T.F. (who figure together as the Professor). I can honestly say they changed everything; they removed the claim to decipher, instead to (dis)entangle, to refuse to fix meaning (which, in the end, is to 'refuse God and his hypostases – reason, science, law'). They ensured this Text cannot be authored. (By chance one of them later told me that they had had an affair, though 'there was no penetration').

I was introduced to the anachronistic joy of 8mm film and the beguiling 'truths' of three quite different, but not unlikely bedfellows: Barthes, Bataille and Bowie. I still recall, vividly, being firmly engrossed in reading, hanging onto my seat with my buttocks, as the bus from college (a Routemaster with an open back) went screaming along the suburban streets of South London. I never fully understood what I was reading, but it was suggestive of the 'activity of production' that has never since ceased. Sometimes, after Bowie, I can't help wondering if the *whole* world is in fact queer ('…sometimes, but always in vain').

During my time at college, I also met a talkative woman at my photography night-class. She was at least 10 years older, faintly alluring, yet detached. One evening she confided she was only taking the course so as to prepare artworks that would be 'really shocking'. These were the days when art was predictably all about new sensations. I was hooked, of course, but she never would say just what she had planned. We soon lost touch and so I don't know what she ever went onto make (if anything). I can't say there has ever been anything I've come across that might suggest she was successful. In fact, I must confess, I've never been shocked since, at least not by artworks of any kind, nor even, I might add, by the events of 9/11 (which I must stress I hardly think was anything like the sort of thing the woman had in mind).

When 'they' go low, so I've been told, *go high*. But to go high is sometimes to go low, to go underground. The sensationalists, from the point of view of appearance and brilliance, are like eagles: virile; of uncontested glamour. As Bataille writes: '…the eagle has formed an alliance with the sun, which castrates all that enters into conflict with it (Icarus, Prometheus, the Mithraic bull). Politically the eagle is identified with imperialism … with the unconstrained development of individual authoritarian power'. Meanwhile, ongoing, is the work of the mole, whose quiet revolution 'hollows out chambers in a decomposed soil repugnant to the delicate nose of the utopians'. As Marx put it: 'In history as in nature, decay is the laboratory of life'. Through the mole's churning of the soil can be heard the plurality of meanings, which is not to say merely the co-existence of meanings, but the interrelatedness of things (how all things are soiled). The Text that precedes has as much been 'read' by its author as it can be by its readers. All its incidents are half-identifiable: 'they come from codes which are known but their combination is unique'. So, the Text, as Barthes describes, is seemingly 'semelfactive (this rendering illusory any inductive-deductive silence of text - no "grammar" of the text) and nevertheless woven entirely with citations, references, echoes, cultural languages (what language is not?), antecedent or contemporary, which cut across it through and through in a vast stereophony'.

I should say, then, there are no origins, no sources, but rather all run through the other. Many song-lines, for example, play through the Text. Music, itself, gives us a glimpse into the structure of how we 'read' texts temporally and through polyphony. And in itself Bataille's *Histoire de l'Oeil* is made up of many parts. Originally published in 1928 under the pseudonym of Lord Auch (with later versions published in 1940, 1941, and 1967 - the latter, the final, posthumous version, properly attributes Bataille for the first time). For me the obvious 'source' was the English version, *Story of the Eye*, translated by Joachim Neugroschal (1982); yet its rendering as *A Tale of Satisfied Desire*, translated by Audiart (1953), gives us another take. We are often told different translations help to keep each other in check, but equally what Bataille leaves out in the various versions is as informative as is how the different translations go about their work.

As things progressed all number of citations were woven into and emerged out from the Text, often, but not always, indicated by the use of italics or quote marks. Some of the materials are obvious, such as Henri Barbusse's *L'Enfer*, H.G. Wells' 'The Country of the Blind' (and, less obviously, *War of the Worlds*), and Marcel Proust's *In Search of Lost Time*. As well as Bataille's *The Tears of Eros*, Walter Benjamin's *Arcades Project* (and 'Berlin Childhood around 1900'), Friedrich Nietzsche's *Thus Spoke Zarathustra*, Jacques Lacan's *The Four Fundamental Concepts of Psychoanalysis*, several works by Jean Baudrillard, Michel Foucault's *The Order of Things*, along with also Jacques Derrida's *Memoirs of the Blind* and *The Postcard*, Hélène Cixous' *Neutre* and *Love Itself in the Letter Box*, and Monique Wittig's *The Lesbian Body*. Some of the points of reference are more technical: Jean-Paul Sartre's *Nausea*, Justin Lorentzen's 'Snapshots: Notes on Myth, Memory and Technology', Roland Barthes' *The Pleasure of the Text* and *Carnets du voyage en Chine*, Simone de Beauvoir's *Brigitte Bardot*, Donald Winnicott's *Playing and Reality* (and 'The

Capacity to be Alone'), Victor Burgin's *The Remembered Film*, Derrida's *Of Grammatology*, Sal Renshaw's *The Subject of Love*, Julia Kristeva's *About Chinese Women*, Norman Bryson's 'The Gaze in the Expanded Field', and Keiji Nishitani's *Religion and Nothingness*. Also, Baudrillard's collaboration with Luc Delahaye for *L'Autre*; and of course, Roland Barthes' 'The Eiffel Tower'. Nonetheless, others came as more of a *pleasure* and surprise: Virginia Woolf's *The Waves*, D.H. Lawrence's *Sons and Lovers*, Umberto Eco's *The Name of the Rose*, André Malraux's *Le Musée imaginaire de la sculpture mondiale*, and Philippe Sollers' *Event*. In addition, numerous visual references and artworks circulate the Text, but which are mostly too self-evident to need be named. Finally, I might add, Marq Smith's rather brilliant article, 'DisORIENTation: travels through blackness', undoubtedly cast a long shadow throughout the writing, yet rather prophetically never seemed to *enter* the Text, despite various attempts.

In the end, it is uncomfortable to make such a list since it is of course inexhaustible. I choose not to linger over such matters, for I have long since relinquished any sense of order or authorship. There is no way I could restore the true magnitude of such an inheritance, instead I can only seek to transform things, make them unrecognisable, at least at first glance, and in part it has been a necessary process of deformation, to allow these sources to acquire new lewd meanings, so as to disorientate and make new. To return to Barthes's thoughts on the preparation on the novel, he reminds us: '*reading* is a metonymical, all-consuming activity; you're gradually pulling the entire continuum {*nappe*} of culture toward you; as into the sea at high tide, you plunge into the Imaginary of Culture, into the chorus, the polyphony of a thousand other voices, to which I add my own: a book.' But, more fittingly, he punctuates this 'theoretical' account with a more visceral image:

> When I was a child, I'd see women all around me
> obsessed by the risk of getting a nick in their
> knitted stockings (no nylon), causing a loose
> thread to suddenly start unravelling down the
> length of the stocking, and I can still picture that
> slightly vulgar but necessary gesture whereby they
> would moisten a finger in their mouths before
> applying it to the loose thread—checking the
> ladder by cementing it with saliva … This is what
> Writing is like: a finger pressed onto the culture's
> Imaginary … in a way, writing is the
> immobilization of culture (perhaps so that it can
> append itself to it) … Whence, I believe, a sort of
> necessity, from the moment you undertake the
> Work, of putting a stop to reading, of effecting a
> reading Blank.

For all its vulgarity, *Pornography of the Gaze* is a chance to put
a stop to reading, to be *blank*, and impressively so.

Barthes / Bataille

Sunil Manghani

Barthes / Bataille

…there is an alternation of knowledge and value,
rest from one in the other, according to a kind of
amorous rhythm. And here, in short, is what writing
is, and singularly the writing of essays (we are
speaking of Bataille): the amorous rhythm of
science and value: heterology, delight.

- Roland Barthes, *Outcomes of the Text*

Why did Roland Barthes choose to write about Georges
Bataille? In terms of themes, subject matter and imagery
there would appear to be some distance between them.

Bataille chose to write about death, violence, eroticism, blindness and transgression, while Barthes is known for his interest in popular culture, hedonism, the pleasures of the text, the brevity of haiku, the 'wonders' of Japan, and mourning – and all with a certain underlying 'discretion'. Historically, between Bataille's *Story of the Eye*, from 1928, and Barthes' acute commentary upon it, in his well-known essay 'Metaphor of the Eye' from 1962, there are clear differences.

Bataille emerged as a notable figure of the surrealist movement and comes from a generation of writers and artists directly affected by the First World War. A stark visual experience is attributed to this period, leading to whole new preoccupations and perturbations. 'I MYSELF AM WAR', Bataille writes in a text on joy before death: 'There are explosives everywhere that will soon blind me. I laugh when I think that my eyes persist in demanding objects that do not destroy them'. By the time Barthes publishes his essay in 1962 (a year after Bataille's death), there is a very different outlook. The post-War period had given rise to a growing middle class, increased affluence and new cultural configurations. The main intellectual debates of the period now centred around structuralism and the linguistic turn in philosophy. It is generally in this context that the Bataille we evoke today properly emerges.

In his lifetime, Bataille was not widely read, yet he gained significant posthumous interest in the 1960s following his 'discovery' among a generation of post-structuralist thinkers (Barthes included among them). In keeping with Martin Jay's thesis of 'downcast eyes' (the denigration of vision in 20th-century French thought) it was Bataille's counter-Enlightenment critique of vision that was 'a vital inspiration' to the poststructuralists' own insistent interrogation.[1] Certainly this can be seen in Barthes' commentary on *Story of the Eye*, and is also picked up in a range of scholarly writings around the time of the novel's republication in 1967. Barthes' essay was a key early text offering clarity upon Bataille. It fits with Barthes' later account of Sade, whom he argued offered a *system* of meaning of greater importance than the pornographic subject matter it employs.

Yet, such clarity would be anathema to Bataille. He argues, for example, against Jean-Paul Sartre's desire for the lucid and reflexive mediation of a message (as associated with committed writing). Instead, Bataille argued that true communication demands obscurity. 'Communication, in my sense', he writes, in *Literature and Evil*, 'is never stronger than when communication, in the weak sense, the sense of the profane language, or, as Sartre says, of prose which makes us and the others appear penetrable, fails and becomes the equivalent of darkness'.

Nevertheless, to judge Barthes only on his 'lucid' exposition of *Story of the Eye* would be to miss a closer connection. His reference to the work as poem rather than novel is significant. Sartre privileges prose over poetry (the latter being a thing in itself, rather than the mediation of something). In *What is Literature?*, Sartre describes poets as those who 'refuse to *utilize* language'. It is the utilization of language that Bataille refuses, arguing instead that it is through the excess of language that we are able to be free, or at least seek to break from what he refers to as our restricted economy (or what Barthes calls the *doxa*). It is a position that equates with Barthes' infamous remark that all language, or specifically *the performance of a language system*, is fascist. Furthermore, while Barthes writes very little on poetry, it is his characterization of modern poetry as 'a quality *sui generis* and without antecedents … no longer an attribute, but a substance' (in *Writing Degree Zero*), which aligns closely with Bataille's conception and 'operation' of language.

It is worth noting that Bataille's *The Impossible* (which presents both an erotic narrative and an essay on poetry) was originally titled 'The Hatred of Poetry'. The operative word is 'of' – rather than read this as Bataille holding a hatred of poetry, it is his interest in the 'hatred' or subversion that can *come of* poetry that is the point. His argument is against 'beautiful poetry', and in favour of a subversive poetry: 'if there is no subversion, poetry stays trapped in the realm of everyday activity, which reduces it to the status of merely "beautiful poetry", that is, pure rhetoric, or poetic verbiage'.[2] Bataille's distinction between beautiful and subversive poetry echoes that of Barthes' distinction of the classical and modern.

Barthes' *other* essay on Bataille, 'Outcomes of the Text', has received less attention, but here Barthes' reading of both Bataille and 'what writing is' becomes more salient. Written in 1972, a decade on from his first essay on Bataille, the account reveals a connection to Bataille that underpins much of Barthes' thinking throughout his career. Indeed, a thread can be traced from Barthes' first book, *Writing Degree Zero*, through to his final lecture courses, notably *The Neutral*, given at the Collège de France between 1977–8. It is worth noting, in this later period, Barthes takes up a regular practice of painting, as a private and 'amateur' practice, which we can read in a Bataillean fashion as 'expenditure', as surplus to Barthes' own writing and thinking. The paintings are a form of 'squandering' and 'drift'. In taking this broader view of Barthes, the contention is that, despite differing styles and sensibilities, both Barthes and Bataille gather upon similar philosophical concerns, and that, crucially, looking *between* them provides an opportunity to contend with the difficult position they both sought to take up vis-à-vis neutrality and heterology, respectively. Bataille's reference to a 'general economy', as the rejection of what he referred to as our 'restricted economy', and Barthes' frequent formulation of, or search for, a 'third' term help us to locate certain commonalities of 'Barthes/Bataille'. Neither holds a singular position, rather they both present a sliding or 'baffling' form of structuralism, which is against categories, and is instead attuned to intensities (as expressions that defy classification). In conclusion, the 'practice of writing' for both Barthes and Bataille is framed as an ethical response, pertaining to what might be referred to as the 'preparations' of knowledge; a judiciousness towards what forms *in* and *around* knowledge, allowing as much for pauses as the possibilities of thought.

An Eye for an Eye

Barthes' 'The Metaphor of the Eye' offers an exemplary commentary on Bataille's *Story of the Eye*. The story is not of the main characters, Barthes argues, but of an object, the eye, or more particularly its movement from image to image. As such, it is not a novel, he claims, but a poem:

> The novelistic imagination is 'probable': the novel is what, all things considered, might happen ... the poetic imagination, on the contrary, is improbable: ... the poem alone can designate; the novel proceeds by aleatory combinations of real elements; the poem by an exact and complete exploration of virtual elements.

Establishing Bataille's story as a 'poem' allows Barthes to

focus upon the text as 'operation', rather than as simply form and content. A structuralist account is provided, looking at 'arrangement and selection, syntagm and paradigm'. In particular, Barthes takes the pairings metonymy and metaphor. Of the latter, the Eye is traced through various substitutions (eye, egg, testicles, i.e. as ocular globes), which in turn leads to liquid forms (tears, milk, egg yolk, sperm, urine). It is 'the very mode of the moist', Barthes suggests, where metaphor is the richer; 'from damp to runny, it is all the varieties of the inundant which complete the original metaphor of the globe; objects apparently quite remote from the eye are suddenly caught up in the metaphoric chain'. Reference to 'dampness' recurs in Barthes' Neutral lectures, which is symptomatic of his interest in that which falls outside of systems of signification (i.e. there is an indeterminacy to dampness, that is neither fully wet nor dry). It is not so much the specific metaphors that count (which are held within sign systems), but their *movement*, within the 'space' in which metaphors metamorphose.

The eye as globe also serves as a reminder of the circularity of meanings, the fact there is no originary sign. *Story of the Eye* is 'a perfectly spherical metaphor': one signifier is always contingent with the next.

> [It is] not a 'profound' work: everything is given on the surface and without hierarchy, the metaphor is displayed in its entirety; circular and explicit, it refers to no secret: . . . an open literature which is situated beyond any decipherment and which only a formal criticism can – at a great distance – accompany.

However, it is not just on the paradigmatic axis that

Bataille's text produces its 'poetic' effects. Its metaphoric substitutions are also 'crossed' syntagmatically. The breaking of an egg, the poking of an eye, become the breaking of an eye, the poking of an egg. In reference to Roman Jakobson's opposition of metaphor (as similarity) and metonymy (as contiguity), it is the latter, Barthes argues, that gives rise to Bataille's eroticism. Metaphor *varies* the objects, it 'manifests a regulated difference among them', while metonymy *exchanges* them: 'properties are no longer divided: to flow, to sob, to urinate, to ejaculate — these are a vacillating meaning. . . [signifying] in the manner of a vibration which always produces the same sound'. Reference here to 'vibration' again can be shown to resonate with Barthes' later writings on the Neutral as a spectrum or degrees of meaning, as intensities, rather than as categories. Metonymic exchange, Barthes explains, enables the transgression of values, 'for metonymy is precisely a forced syntagm, the violation of a signifying limit of space; it permits, on the very level of discourse, a counterdivision of objects, usages, meanings, spaces, and properties'.

While Barthes' analysis of *Story of the Eye* has drawn criticism over the years, the essay leads to a significant resolution with its closing comparison of Bataille and Sade:

> Sade's erotic language has no other connection than that of his century, it is writing [*une écriture*]; Bataille's erotic language is connoted by Georges Bataille's very being, it is a style; between the two, something is born, something which transforms every experience into a warped language and which is literature.

Barthes' use of the word 'style' is to be understood in terms of the body (though notably not the gendered body). As he outlines in *Writing Degree Zero*, style is not something the writer chooses, but is of the accumulations of the body. It is only through writing (*écriture*) that the strictures of language and the body (style) can be outplayed. This is Barthes' final argument as regards Bataille. His 'warped language' is the new force of Writing, which presses against or outplays the codifications of Literature. Of course, as Barthes' thesis in *Writing Degree Zero* acknowledges, all writing will eventually be subsumed within the categories of Literature, but at least the *practice* of writing is an open site of exchange. It is worth noting that Bataille does not figure in *Writing Degree Zero*, yet, according to Barthes himself, this is merely due to an 'ignorance' of his work at the time. By inference, then, Barthes acknowledges Bataille a notable absence in the book.

Of course, there is always a dilemma in placing the writing of Bataille, since he was wary of *both* the rejection and the enthusiastic appropriation of his work. In 'The Use-Value of D.A.F. de Sade', he looks to uphold the 'scandal' of Sade's writing. Counter-intuitively, he suggests those who receive Sade's work with indignation and protest better uphold the value of his work, more so that his admirers, who make him 'acceptable', part of a 'thoroughly literary enterprise'. Bataille's argument with many in the Surrealist movement (notably André Breton) is this literary appropriation of Sade, which is similarly a concern held over the reception of Bataille's work. Rejection and appropriation are arguably two sides of the same coin; both share a form of control over the transgressive writer. Yet, equally, neither can take complete control. There remain 'unassimilable elements', which underlie his practice of writing. Rather than making Sade acceptable (part of the canon), we need to accept the full force of his writing (in the same way as those who reject him for his perversity). *An eye for an eye*: it is to make a reading that allows for a 1:1 association with the text, *not* its approximation or domestication (which is to recall Bataille's 'hatred' of poetry, the 'impossibility' of language). As has been said: 'Bataille's objective is to expose all writing to the violent excitation of the heterogeneous and so to force us to confront the impossibility at the heart of thought'.[3]

In connection with Barthes, it is worth remembering he opens *Writing Degree Zero* with reference to a journalist writing in *Le Père Duchêne* who would always begin his articles with a series of obscenities. 'These improprieties had no real meaning', Barthes explains, 'but they had significance.' They embodied a revolutionary situation through 'a mode of writing whose function is no longer only communication or expression, but the imposition of something beyond language'.

It is the working in and against structures of signification that is most pertinent about Sade and Bataille's writings and draws a line between them (and which brings us to the connection with Barthes). As Susan Sontag notes: 'despite the obvious differences of scale and finesse of execution, the conceptions of Sade and Bataille have some resemblances. Like Bataille, Sade was not so much a sensualist as someone with an intellectual project: to explore the scope of transgression'.[4] Breton famously asserted that Bataille thought too much to be a surrealist, but arguably that is what makes him of continued interest today. It is the 'scope' of transgression, not transgressions in themselves, that is at stake and which, importantly, suggests a *rigorous* inquiry. As has been said of Foucault's account of Bataille, for example, 'transgression does not overcome limits. . . but shows that what we are, our being, depends on the existence of limits'.[5] Thus, at root, Barthes' reading of *Story of the Eye* holds true. With both these thinkers there is a (post-)structuralist project in play (Bataille through his reading of the proto-structuralist Mauss; Barthes through his reading of Saussure, Lévi-Strauss, Jakobson). Yet perhaps attention upon the story of the 'eye' is too loaded. To get closer to a 1:1 reading, to locate the more 'radical' nature of their respective projects, we might avert our gaze, to look below the line; to turn from the nexus of the eye to the prosaic big toe (and Barthes' fragmentary essay that presents its 'outcomes').

Operation Formless

Barthes' later essay on Bataille, 'Outcomes of the Text', is more in keeping with Bataille's avant-garde writing and his compiling of an alternative dictionary in *Documents*. Barthes' text is composed as a series of fragments, 'in a more or less emphatic state of severance from each other' and presented in alphabetical order so as to be 'both an order and a disorder, an order stripped of meaning, the degree zero of order'. In suggesting these fragments are 'outcomes' of the text, we can suppose there is a play on Jacques Derrida's famous remark that there is no outside-text. These fragments are commentaries on Bataille's consideration (or desire) to reach an outside or periphery of meaning (as well as a sexual connotation, or 'outcome' as *jouissance*). In this case, Barthes' text is a reading of Bataille's 'The Big Toe'. In his opening lines, Bataille remarks how the big toe is the most singularly unique part of the human body, while equally a great leveller; its position upon the ground gives a 'baseness', it is horizontal, material, not vertical and ideal. In casting our gaze downward, upon the horizontal, as Barthes explains, we encounter a wider, heterogeneous field of knowledge:

In Bataille's text, there are many 'poetic' codes: thematic (high/low, noble/ignoble, light/muddy), amphibological (the word *erection*, for instance), metaphorical ('man is a tree'); there are also codes of knowledge: anatomical, zoological, ethnological, historical. Of course, the text *exceeds* knowledge – by value; but even within the field of knowledge, there are differences of pressure, of 'seriousness', and these differences produce a heterology.

Of course, it is not to suggest *Story of the Eye* does not present similar pressures on knowledge to produce a heterology. Running through these various texts of Bataille is an interest in their 'operation' (which goes beyond questions of form and content). Barthes' key observation of *Story of the Eye*, for example, is to identify the 'eye' with imagination itself, 'not its product but its substance'. To elucidate this point, we can refer to W.J.T. Mitchell's account of the image as something that is not necessarily tangible or visible. In Milton's *Paradise Lost* there is the evocative phrase 'in their looks divine', which is to deliberately confuse, or indeed conjoin the visible and invisible, the pictorial and the spiritual. Mitchell explains how everything pivots upon the word 'looks', which may refer to outward appearance as much as the intangible sense of 'looks' as a quality of one's gaze.[6] Bataille's metonymic writing in *Story of the Eye* can be said to operate similarly, i.e. to 'look' both ways, offering in Barthes' words again 'a counterdivision of objects, usages, meanings, spaces and properties'.

Yet, still, there is something about the eye as an object that is hard to divide. The problem is made apparent, with Luis Buñuel and Salvador Dali's film *Un Chien Andalou*, which Bataille viewed favourably. While conceptually the film's famous and shocking scene of the cutting of the eye *signified* a cut in the 'visual field', it nonetheless remains a singly difficult image. As Bataille notes, Buñuel remained sick for a week after filming the scene. Both *Un Chien Andalou* and *Story of the Eye* reject the penetrating gaze, the idea that it is possible to *see through* things, to realize a true (Platonic) meaning 'behind' what is shown. Both eschew the (hierarchical) distinctions of surface and depth. As cited above, Barthes 'profoundly' notes *Story of the Eye* is 'not a "profound" work'. Yet, the problem remains: we still cannot take our eye off *the* shot of the slicing of the eye (the 'money shot' of the avant-garde). We tend only to look one way (if we don't look away), returning always to this moment, not where it might take us. We cannot help but replace an eye for a (mutilated) eye.

Bataille's essay 'The Big Toe' is again prompted by the visual image, but in a quite different way. It is a text that accompanies a series of three arresting photographic close-ups of big toes, by the photographer J.A. Boiffard, which appeared in the sixth issue of *Documents* (in 1929). The use of the close-up, of strong lighting, tight framing (presenting the toe in isolation) and enlargement (each image scaled larger than life, as a full-page image), had the effect of both documenting the human toe, yet equally making it somehow 'other'. Unlike Bataille's narrative of the eye (that is taken out and inserted in different ways; that has its own 'story'), the images by Boiffard are supposed to offer a more direct encounter with our own eyes. We are 'seduced in a base manner', writes Bataille, 'without transpositions and to the point of screaming, opening [our] eyes wide: opening them wide, then, before a big toe'. Interestingly, Bataille takes this to be against 'poetic concoctions', which he suggests are 'nothing but a diversion' (though again, poetry here is not the same as Bataille's notion of the 'hatred' of poetry). Instead, we ourselves enter the 'substance' of seeing rather than viewing its product (or empirical outcome). Of course, we might argue 'an image stands as the conclusion of Bataille's thoughts – possibly because that is where thought slips away, living on in its own death'.[7]

While sharing much with the surrealist project, Bataille imposed a subversive power that could undermine *all* meaning. So, while the surrealists' work might present a heterogeneity of the real, it would point to a 'unity at another level – that of the subject's lost but recoverable subjectivity'.[8] By contrast, in Bataille's project, as evidenced in *Documents*, 'disunity presides ... the juxtaposition of radically different and incommensurable images... insists on relationships that serve to undermine the integrity of the entities caught up in a violent process of dislocation, rather than pointing to a higher level of interpretation'.[9] However, rather than focus on the notion of 'disunity', suggestive of a binary order/disorder, Bataille's project can be understood more particularly as an opening out of the fields of knowledge, of the *othering* of knowledge, or heterology. This is certainly evident in the language of 'The Big Toe', which explicitly plays upon the distinction of high and low, ideal (vision) and base ('grounded' by our feet). However, Bataille is not merely presenting a critique of the longstanding mind/body dichotomy. In his writing on the eye and toe, his heterology is *operative*, a notion that is developed further in reference to his interest of *informe* (formless), notably in his essay on the painter Édouard Manet.

In a catalogue essay for the Manet retrospective in 1982 (Paris and New York), Françoise Cachin argues there are broadly two responses to the painter's work. On the one hand formalist, concerned with painterly values and technique, and on the other, a consideration of the 'scandal' of Manet's subject matter.[10] At first glance, Bataille's essay on Manet appears to sit within the formalist concerns, yet this position is based on Bataille's précis of André Malraux. Instead, Bataille suggests of a 'disinterested' point of view. In *Shootings of May Third* (1812), he suggests Francisco Goya captured 'the blinding, instantaneous flash of death, a thunderbolt of sight-destroying intensity, brighter than any known light'. While Manet's rendering in *The Execution of Maximilian* (1867) presents something altogether different, having 'wrung the last drop of meaning out of the subject'. '*Maximilian*', he writes, 'reminds us of a tooth deadened by novocaine; we get the impression of an all-engulfing numbness, as if a skilful practitioner had radically cured painting of a centuries-old ailment: chronic eloquence.' Bataille goes on to offer further 'blithe' descriptors of Manet's work, suggesting he poses models, for example, 'as if they were about to "buy a bunch of radishes" … There remain a variety of colour patches and the impression that the subject ought to have induced an emotional reaction but has failed to do so – the curious impression of absence.' The 'effect' of absence gives rise to what Bataille calls an 'imponderable plenitude', which he argues is 'perhaps essential to what modern man really is, supremely, silently, when he consents to reject the pompous rhetoric that seems to give sense to everyday life, but which actually falsifies our feelings and commits them to a ludicrous abjection'.

Manet, according to Bataille's account, breaks with ideological and formal codes; his subject is not located 'anywhere', it is rootless. And indeed, for Bataille 'it is this uprooting, which he also calls slippage, that is Manet's "secret": the true goal is to "disappoint expectation"'.[11] In tracing Malraux's account, Bataille pushes further, suggesting Malraux 'fails to define what gives *Olympia*. . . its value *as an operation*'. It is this 'operation' of slippage that is also to be understood in what Bataille calls the *informe* (formless), and which underlines the 'general movement of Bataille's thought, which he liked to call a "scatology" or "heterology"'.[12] Bataille's account of *informe* is given in just 15 lines, as part of the 'critical dictionary' published in *Documents*; arguably 'one of the most effective ... acts of sabotage against the academic world and the spirit of the system'.[13] Its effectiveness is derived from its 'formal ruse', which turns the conventional upon its head:

> The whole of Bataille's writing rests on such apparent non sequiturs (which he calls 'ink spots' or 'quacks' in his essay 'The Language of Flowers,' which gave André Breton heartburn): 'bunch of radishes,' 'the tooth deadened novocaine,' in all his text we find these rude belches, the virulence of which owes much to irony. The 'dictionary' accumulates them, functioning, so to speak, as one big quack: nothing stirred up Bataille's blasphemous energy more than the definition of words, which he calls their 'mathematical frock coat'.[14]

The metonymic is seemingly pushed more to an absurdist mode (parallels have been noted with Beckett), but still the writing maintains a contiguity, a way of moving one thing to (and against) another. It is a means of working against and exposing our restrictive economy (or the *doxa*, to use Barthes' favoured term). The phrase 'frock coat' (itself an 'ink spot'), is reference to our restricted way of thinking and knowing the world. It is a phrase picked out from Bataille's 15-line statement:

A dictionary begins when it no longer gives the meaning of words, but their tasks. Thus *formless* is not only an adjective having a given meaning, but a term that serves to bring things down in the world, generally requiring that each thing have its form. What it designates has no rights in any sense and gets itself squashed everywhere, like a spider or an earthworm. In fact, for academic men to be happy, the universe would have to take shape. All of philosophy has no other goal: it is a matter of giving a frock coat to what is a mathematical frock coat. On the other hand, affirming that the universe resembles nothing and is only *formless* amounts to saying that the universe is something like a spider or spit.

Despite, or indeed due to its brevity, this statement can be read as Bataille's manifesto on heterology. The idea that 'each thing have its form' suggests a massive taxonomy, but of course the very idea of a 'taxonomy' (of imposing a system of meaning) is contra to Bataille's position. It is to give shape to the universe, when he suggests of a shapeless, or formless array. Politically, or at least ethically, allowing for the formless is to allow for all and sundry; the things that we usually miss or elide – the spider that hides in amongst the dust, or the spit that is quashed under foot, or looked upon as abject.

We need to hold onto Bataille's actual operation of writing, one that is 'baffling'. As he puts it in the opening of his statement, the 'dictionary begins when it no longer gives the meaning of words, but their tasks'. There is a connection with Barthes' writing, including his early and arguably most well-known book, *Mythologies*. Here, we should not be drawn to the semiological terminology, as located in the book's closing essay (nor the pseudo-theoretical terms encountered later on, such as the 'obtuse meaning', or the 'punctum', etc.). Instead, we can linger over the journalistic texts that make up the bulk of the book, including, for example, the seemingly benign 'Operation Margarine'. There is a myth attached to margarine, which Barthes derives from the publicity of *Astra* margarine, whereby prejudice against it (as being inferior to butter) stands in the way of progress and common sense and will literally 'cost you dearly'. However, this is not what the article seeks to unravel. Rather it assumes we *already* share in this knowledge, and as such can use the myth of margarine as an effective means to expose something of greater significance.

The text is actually concerned with how the 'Established Order' (those in power, etc.) can turn their weaknesses to advantage. He gives two specific examples, how the army and church both openly note their failings, yet in doing so herald their continued importance and virtue. 'It is a kind of homeopathy', he suggests, 'One inoculates the public with a contingent evil to prevent or cure an essential one'. The argument is that we put up with ongoing, seemingly temporary complaints (or 'contingent' wrongdoing), in order to uphold the idea of some greater good. He ends the article with the allusion to margarine, which in all its banality would seem to have the effect of both inoculating us against Barthes' own critical argument, yet equally seeming to expose the fact we were aware of the mythological construct all along. Thus, Barthes writes: 'It is well worth the price of an immunization. What does it matter, *after all*, if margarine is just fat, when it goes further than butter, and costs less? What does it matter, *after all*, if Order is a little brutal or a little blind, when it allows us to live cheaply?'. This is the 'operation' noted in the title. He manages to link the exposing of what he takes to be a deep-level flaw in society with the simple act of spreading margarine on one's toast at the breakfast table. He achieves a way of 'bringing home' to us an otherwise abstract, political problem. It is perhaps no such surprise then, at his inaugural lecture at the Collège de France, Barthes claimed the semiologist needs to be 'an artist' playing with signs 'as with a conscious decoy, whose fascination he savours and wants to make others savour and understand'. The sign for this artist 'is always immediate, subject to the kind of evidence that leaps to the eyes, like a trigger of the imagination', which is why semiology in this case 'is not a hermeneutics: it paints more than it digs'. The *operation* of Barthes/Bataille is indeed one of 'painting', of writing (fiction), not digging.

Déjouer: General/Neutral Economy

The underlying thread of the preceding account works upon a trajectory from Barthes' first book, *Writing Degree Zero*, to his late lecture course *The Neutral*, through which Bataille offers a way of thinking about both a philosophical position (or an a-philosophical position) and writing *as practice*, relating to a mode of writing as being operational. These points can be drawn together to suggest an ethics of knowledge. Barthes' original reference to 'degree zero' is in the service of trying to secure *writing* as a defining feature of literature, as something that can outplay the strictures of language and style. He turns attention to neutral, colourless writing, exemplified at the time by novelists such as Camus and Robbe-Grillet (to whom could be added Bataille as already suggested). Of course, according to Barthes' own thesis, 'zero degree' soon becomes its own genre, subsumed within the 'culture industry'. It is not until his penultimate lecture course, published posthumously as *The Neutral*, that Barthes returns critically to the phrase 'zero degree'. In these lectures, taking a wide-ranging and metonymic approach, he draws up a series of dossiers on topics as various as benevolence, weariness, tact, damp, sleep, retreat, arrogance, through which he presents various 'figures' of the Neutral, putting together what he describes as a 'dictionary not of definitions but of twinklings [*scintillations*]'. There is a parallel here to Bataille's dictionary of words as tasks, and his mode of writing through apparent non-sequiturs (his 'ink spots' and 'quacks'). In referring to weariness, for example, Barthes says it is 'not coded, is not received … [it] always functions in language as a mere metaphor, a sign without referent'. This is in contrast to depression and mourning, he notes, which have been inscribed with 'social claims'. He suggests the following experiment:

> …draw up a table of received (credible) excuses: you want to cancel a lecture, an intellectual task: what excuses will be beyond suspicion, beyond reply? Weariness? Surely not. Flu? Bad, banal. A surgical operation? Better, but watch out for the vengeance of fate! Cf. the way society codifies mourning in order to assimilate it: after a few weeks, society will reclaim its rights, will no longer accept mourning as a state of exception…

What interests Barthes about weariness is that it is not codified, it cannot be assimilated in discourse (connection can be made to Bataille's *Guilty*, which, rather than portray a heroic account of the war, speaks of drift, distraction and disengagement – sentiments that again cannot easily be assimilated, certainly in the context of the Second World

War). Thus, for Barthes, weariness is unclassifiable:

> ...without premises, without place, socially untenable → whence Blanchot's (weary!) cry: 'I don't ask that weariness be done away with. I ask to be led back to a region where it might be possible to be weary.' → Weariness = exhausting claim of the individual body that demands the right to social repose (that sociality in me rest a moment [...]). In fact, weariness = an intensity: society doesn't recognize intensities.

We can begin to see how Barthes' account of weariness relates to Bataille's critique of restrictive economy, with the Neutral leading us similarly to a sense of 'general economy'. Both are against the conception of society based only on (a restrictive definition of) economics. Barthes' lament that we cannot simply call in sick because we feel weary is to raise questions about our relationship (and alienation) to economic labour. And more than that, his description of 'intensities' (as the measure of the Neutral) tallies with Bataille's privileging of excess and specifically with his reference to 'unproductive expenditures': those activities, for Bataille, that are not 'reducible to processes of production and conservation'. Weariness does not lead to anything; it does not give us profit. Instead, it is an energy (albeit a fading energy) that is on a par with Bataille's understanding of economy as energy and expenditure. His particular interest in solar energy as the 'source of life's exuberant development', as an 'open system', and in effect a 'free gift' ('The sun gives without ever receiving'), is something we cannot describe or classify, but is an intensity, an underlying force. Fundamentally, the 'solar economy', as Bataille conceives it, positions humans not as 'wasteful' beings (as in *utilizing* the planet's resources), but more simply as the sun's waste product. We are its outcome, its luxury, and we continue to profligate because of it. We *are* expenditure, yet we fail to recognize this through our own follies of restrictive economy and codified knowledge structures (that define utility, not intensities). According to Bataille, restrictive economy, 'the sphere dominated by economics', for example, 'consists of all that is deemed normal, all that seeks to make society controllable'. Outside of which is excess: 'eroticism, death, festivals, transgression, drunkenness, laughter, the dissolution of truth and knowledge',[15] a list to which we might readily append the Neutral (or at least see it as an expression of dissolution). This is the general economy, but importantly, 'the general economy is also the process whereby the homogeneous realm interacts with excessive phenomena'.[16] In other words, we cannot view restrictive and general economies as separate entities – the former sits within the latter. In Barthes' terms, as previously suggested, restrictive economy equates in many respects, to what he calls *doxa*, while the Neutral, by contrast, is his way of conceiving of general economy. Indeed, the open structure of his lecture course, as a series of randomly ordered dossiers, provides an unfolding array of 'excesses' or figures of intensities. And similarly, it is the interaction of the *doxa* within the Neutral that becomes instructive of how we *choose* to live (which includes, for example, failing to recognize our sense of weariness).

Barthes 'defines' the Neutral as 'that which outplays [*déjoue*] the paradigm, or rather I call Neutral everything that baffles the paradigm. For I am not trying to define a word; I am trying to name a thing: I gather under a name, which here is the Neutral.' There is an important connection with

Bataille's use of *informe*, not least the difficulty in attributing the definite article to these terms. In other words, 'informe' (formless) is not the same as 'formlessness':

> Form itself, however radical, is by definition, and even by self-definition (in modernism), fixed, or at least located. Bataille's informe/formless is something else altogether: in not having an article, it reduces the possibility of becoming an entity … How it works is as a sort of undoing, an undoing which remains even when something takes or is given form.[17]

Similarly, there are no specific examples of the Netural that can hold (take form), but akin to the edge of a black hole (which is otherwise undetectable), Barthes' constellation of various 'figures' clusters around points of significance, which in turn can lead us to renewed questions about how we make meaning in the first place (as we see with the example of weariness). The idea that the Neutral outplays or baffles the paradigm directly echoes Barthes' reading of Bataille in 'Outcomes of the Text', which also adopts the use of the verb 'to baffle'. In commenting on the high/low distinction in 'The Big Toe', Barthes explains how an 'outside' term underlines Bataille's heterology:

> …there is a contradiction, a simple, canonical paradigm between the first two terms: *noble* and *ignoble* … *but* the third term is not regular: *low* is not the neutral term (neither noble nor ignoble), nor is it the mixed term (noble and ignoble). It is an independent term, concrete, eccentric, irreducible: the term of seduction *outside the* (structural) *law*.

Barthes' reference here to a 'neutral term' should not be read in the same sense of the Neutral. Instead, it relates more to the technicalities of rhetoric, of a middle (on the fence) position that ultimately defends the status quo; what he refers to in *Mythologies* as Neither/Nor criticism. Nor should we necessarily read the 'irreducible' as being outside of a structuralist account altogether. *The Neutral* examines various kinds of 'slippage' but maintains a structuralist perspective. He refers, for example, to the lack of opposition between *l* and *r* in Japanese pronunciation as a site of 'no paradigm', and more specifically – drawing upon phonology – he suggests 'the idea of a structural creation that would defeat, annul, or contradict the implacable binarism of the paradigm by means of a third term'. However, again, rather than suggest 'something' that is the Neutral, the meaning of a 'third term' must be taken more as a 'task', as an 'undoing'.

In recounting a scene in which he spills a bottle of ink with the label of 'neutral', Barthes writes: 'I was both punished and disappointed: punished because Neutral spatters and stains (it's a type of dull gray-black); disappointed because Neutral is a color like the others, and for sale'; to which he adds: 'all the more reason for us to go back to discourse, which, at least, cannot say what the Neutral is'. Again, we encounter this need to work within language and its system of signification, but to allow a certain practice of writing to subvert its structures. Thus, the definition of the Neutral remains structural and critical; 'the Neutral doesn't refer to "impressions" of grayness, or "neutrality", of indifference', Barthes writes, 'The Neutral. . . can refer to intense, strong, unprecedented states. "To outplay the paradigm" is an ardent, burning activity'.

Barthes' terms of reference and subject matter are of

course very different in tone to Bataille. When Barthes writes of Japan, of pleasures of the text and the various figures of the Neutral, we might be inclined to view him as the 'light' of Bataille's 'dark' erotic and scatological writing. Yet, in having considered Barthes' interest in *Story of the Eye* and 'The Big Toe', as well as connections between *informe* and Neutral *scintillations* in terms of a recurring writerly method and desire for something more expansive and heterological, structural communalities emerge between the Neutral and Bataille's 'general economy'. For Bataille (and not dissimilar to Barthes' investigations into the Neutral), 'heterology is precisely (and paradoxically) the scientific and rigorous inquiry into those elements necessarily excluded by science and rational thought', the outcome of which is twofold. One result can be 'the ultimate homogenization of heterogeneous elements, in their assimilation to system and order. Here the universe becomes merely another object with clearly defined attributes and heterology remains analogous to other systems of appropriation such as science and philosophy.' Secondly, however, heterology can lead to 'an awareness of the fundamental limit between the heterogeneous and the homogeneous, which, from a theoretical perspective, always remains untraversable'. The point is that heterology essentially only reveals an impossibility, but in doing so helps us to judge our limits and so mark out 'a radical barrier between thought and what is excluded by thought'.[18]

As Barthes remarks in his essay on 'The Big Toe', by proceeding from a 'mixture of knowledges' (which stem from heterology, from understanding the barriers between/beyond thought), it is 'writing' that 'holds in check "the scientific arrogances" … and at the same time sustains an apparent readability.' Barthes deliberately adopts Bataille's phrase (from *Documents*) of 'scientific arrogance', registering a shared target for their criticism. He describes Bataille's writing as 'a burlesque, *heteroclite* knowledge (etymologically: leaning to one side and the other): this is already an operation of knowledge'. While not burlesque, Barthes' Neutral writing is similarly a *heteroclite* knowledge. The idea of which, leaning from one side to the other, begins to suggest of an ability or at least a desire to move in and out of knowledge. Something that operates at both the level of writing and research (and editing). Thus, in 'Outcomes of the Text', under the heading of '*Déjouer* / Baffling', he writes:

> Bataille's text teaches us how to deal with knowledge. We need not reject it. We must even, occasionally, pretend to place it in the forefront. It did not trouble Bataille that the editorial committee of *Documents* consisted of professors, scholars, librarians. Knowledge must be made to appear where it is not expected.

We discern an 'ethics' of knowledge. Neither Barthes nor Bataille are merely trying to subvert or undo knowledge (an act that is quickly subsumed within knowledge itself). They are concerned with the positions we take in leading to (and out from) knowledge. They are interested in the limits, in the 'edges', where things are inevitably *informe*, Neutral (not as forms to be identified, but as positions to be operated, to be untethered or undone). Barthes gives a specific ethical statement in the preliminaries to his Neutral lecture course:

> Transposed to the 'ethical' level: injunctions addressed by the world to 'choose', to produce meaning, to enter conflicts, to 'take responsibility,'

etc. → temptation to suspend, to thwart, to elude the paradigm, its menacing pressure, its arrogance → to exempt meaning → this polymorphous field of paradigm, of conflict avoidance = the Neutral. We are going to grant ourselves the right to treat all conditions, conducts, affects, discourse (with no intention or even possibility of exhaustiveness) as far as they deal with conflict or its release, its parrying, its suspension.

He goes on to describe the Neutral as 'a manner – a free manner – to be looking for my own style of being present to the struggles of my time'. A particular figure of the Neutral is 'Arrogance', the opening of which makes direct reference to Bataille's phrase of 'scientific arrogance'. It is under this heading that Barthes 'gathers all the (linguistic) "gestures" that work as discourses of intimidation, of subjection, of domination, of assertion, of haughtiness'; in other words, all discourses of arrogance (as constitutive of restrictive economy). Within this figure, echoing Bataille's statement on *informe* (and against the philosophical 'goal' for the universe to have to 'take shape'), Barthes includes an entry on the 'concept' (as the defining device of philosophy). Here Barthes places the Neutral on the side of skepticism, which he refers to as being 'invincible' (as we might argue of Bataille's heterology):

Skepticism (to extrapolate: in one sense: the Neutral) is expelled from philosophy, to the extent that it doesn't retain the philosophical 'imprint': the concept … This 'im-position' (at least as seen from the Neutral) = philosophy's arrogance → one can't thus (one couldn't) stay-waft in the space of the Neutral except by staying outside philosophy: but this is something banal … the Neutral cuts itself off from philosophy and from its legitimate victory: it doesn't oppose it but distances itself from it.

Again, we find ideas of proximity to and from knowledge and systems of knowledge (philosophy). Marxism, Barthes suggests, is one example of questioning the concept in a dialectical manner, from within philosophy, but it is Nietzsche whom he considers the 'one who best dismantled. . . the concept'. Indeed, Nietzsche's writings are an important shared reference for both Barthes and Bataille; his critique of the concept underlines both the Neutral and heterology.

> …thus concept: a force that reduces the diverse, the becoming that is the sensible, the *aisthèsis* $\rightarrow$ therefore, if one wants to refuse this reduction, one must say no to the concept, not make use of it. But, then, how to speak, all of us, intellectuals? By metaphors. To substitute metaphor for the concept: to write.

We return again to a practice of writing, the need to infiltrate knowledge; a *virtual* domain that writing can conjure (recalling Barthes' description of *Story of the Eye* as poem, as 'improbable'). Bataille's writing offers 'a different possibility, a different account of general economy as emerging through difference',[19] which similarly we could say of Barthes' Neutral. The suggestion of 'emergence' is significant. One writes within the available terms to nonetheless allow what exists on one side and the other to emerge. And, like Barthes, Bataille (in *The Accursed Share*), is explicit about this as an ethical undertaking: 'Changing from the perspectives of *restrictive* economy to those of *general* economy actually accomplishes a Copernican transformation: a reversal of thinking – and of ethics'. This transformation is to be read not from one economy to another, but from within (a sort of turning inside out). 'It cannot be another type of economy. . . but instead it is the Other of economy'; Bataille's general economy (and what might be called Barthes' Neutral economy) is no longer 'a place to be occupied outside restricted economy but a fleeting and effervescent effect of the swirling turbulence of energy flows that constantly puncture limits, create openings and new limits'.[20]

Preparations of Knowledge

As much as we can read for the political in a practice of writing – of the fictions and figures of both Barthes and Bataille – there is equally an ethics of knowledge: a consideration of how we choose to move in and out of meaning, a form of preparation over knowledge and its scaling. Against the so-called 'knowledge economy' (which Bataille would of course have identified as a restricted economy, being only for accumulation, for capital gain), the emphasis here has been upon a general economy, or a 'neutral economy', to adopt Barthes' terms. Bataille's writings for *Documents*, not least his creation of a dictionary in which the words are not defined but made operative, suggests a different way of *preparing* knowledge, or at least preparing ourselves in the face of it. And again, something similar can be found in Barthes' preparations for his lecture courses; indeed, his final course title was *The Preparation of the Novel*. In terms of their methodologies, one could imagine both writers as entomologists (or Bataille might prefer arachnologist!). They locate and collect the small, seemingly insignificant matter, to then prepare alternative points of reference and altered, re-scaled perspectives. But more than that, they *activate* these 'specimens' (their 'inkblots' and 'traits'). They could be regarded as homeopaths, turning miniscule elements of a 'substance' back upon itself. The 'economies of scale' of our restrictive *doxa* are re-imagined and re-articulated into something much vaster, pluralized. For Barthes, as already noted, it is Bataille who 'teaches us how to deal with knowledge'. In his fragmentary text on 'The Big Toe', Barthes writes:

> Knowledge is fragmented, pluralized, as if the *one* of knowledge were ceaselessly made to divide in two: synthesis is faked, *baffled*; knowledge is there, not destroyed but displaced; its new place is – in Nietzsche's word – that of a *fiction*: meaning precedes and predetermines fact, value precedes and predetermines knowledge ... Knowledge in short, would be an interpretative fiction. Thus, Bataille assures the baffling of knowledge by a fragmentation of the codes, but more particularly by an outburst of value (*noble* and *ignoble*, *seductive* and *deflated*). The role of value is not a role of destruction, nor yet that of dialectization, nor even of subjectivization, it is perhaps, quite simply, a role of *rest*...

The idea of 'rest' Barthes takes directly from Nietzsche:

> ...it suffices for me to know that truth possesses a great *power*. But it must be able to do battle, and it must have an opposition, and from time to time one

must *rest* from it in the non-true. Otherwise, truth would become tedious for us, without savor and without strength, and we would become so as well. . .

In this account, then, writing (as 'fiction') can not only re-order our account of knowledge, it can enable us to take up *other* spaces – spaces which need not necessarily say anything, but simply give the means to pause (again, this is an ethics not a politics of writing). Both Bataille and Barthes were readers of Nietzsche. Both were drawn to what burns, not what sustains. Both engaged in the *writerly*, in *écriture*, as a defiance or baffling of the language and styles that otherwise restrict what we can say.

Between Barthes/Bataille one might place various operators: 'and', 'or', 'not', hyphen, comma, yet the *barre oblique*, the slash, has a particular resonance. It is not to suggest here a split, a dichotomy, but an oscillation, a folding together. It would be too easy, for example, to set them up as dark to light, or weight to weightless. Bataille may have courted the base, the horizontal, while Barthes took delight in a paradigmatic, the 'empty' (zero degree) movement of one term over another (in the haiku, the photograph, in Japanese culture), but in having worked through the connections in their writings, Barthes/Bataille is a dialogue. Together, their structuralist concerns are evoked not to transgress limits (to break out), but to situate precisely upon the limits of transgression. In his autobiography, Barthes recounts a childhood game of 'prisoner's base'. 'What I liked best', he writes, 'was not provoking the other team. . . what I liked best was to free the prisoners – the effect of which was to put both teams back into circulation: the game started over again at zero.' This game is emblematic of the *operations* of both Barthes and Bataille. And we play this game, Barthes suggests, over and over in regular discourse: 'one language has only temporary rights over another; all it takes is for a third language to appear ... The task of this language is to release the prisoners: to scatter the signifieds, the catechisms.' Of course, paradoxically, in order to allow for such critique, there is always the need to let it go: to be only expenditure, not accumulation. Hence, the difficulty for the operations of Barthes/Bataille to be fully written up. Indeed, as a 'final' word, it is perhaps fitting that Barthes' Neutral is never fully authored:

> As a general rule, desire is always marketable: we don't do anything but sell, buy, exchange desires. The paradox of the desire of the Neutral, its absolute singularity, is that it is nonmarketable → people tell me: 'You'll make a book with this course on the Neutral?' All other problems aside ... my answer: No, the Neutral is the unmarketable. And I think of Bloy's words: 'there is nothing perfectly beautiful except what is invisible and above all unbuyable' → 'Invisible'? I would say: 'unsustainable' → We'll have to hold on to the unsustainable for [the duration of the course]: after that, it will fade.

Notes

1. Martin Jay, *Downcast Eyes: The Denigration of Vision in Twentieth-Century French Thought* (Berkeley: University of California Press, 1994), p. 231.
2. Marie-Christine Lala, 'The hatred of poetry in Georges Bataille's

Writing and Thought', in C.B. Gill (ed.) *Bataille: Writing the Sacred* (London: Routledge, 1995), p.108.

3. Benjamin Noys, *Georges Bataille: A Critical Introduction* (London: Pluto Press, 2000), p. 5.

4. Susan Sontag, 'The Pornographic Imagination', in G. Bataille, *Story of the Eye* (London: Penguin, 1982), p.107.

5. Jon Simons, *Foucault and the Political* (London: Routledge, 1995), p. 69.

6. W.J.T. Mitchell, *Iconology: Image, Text, Ideology* (Chicago: University of Chicago Press,1987), pp.35–6.

7. Patrick Crowley and Paul Hegarty (eds.), *Formless: Ways In and Out of Form* (Oxford: Peter Lang, 2005), p.188.

8. Michael Sheringham, *Everyday Life: Theories and Practices from Surrealism to the Present*, (Oxford: Oxford University Press, 2006), p.100; see also: Georges Didi-Huberman, *La Ressemblance informe ou le gai savoir visual de Georges Bataille* (Paris: Macula, 1995).

9. Sheringham, p.100.

10. Françoise Cachin in G. Bataille, *Manet* (London: Macmillan/Editions d'Art Albert Skira, 1983), pp.5–13.

11. Yve-Alain Bois, 'The use value of 'formless'', in Yve-Alain Bois and Rosalind Krauss (eds.), *Formless: A User's Guide* New York: Zone Books, 1997), p.15.

12. ibid.

13. Ibid., p. 16.

14. Ibid.

15. Paul Hegarty, *Georges Bataille: Core Cultural Theorist* (London: Sage, 2000), p.33.

16. Ibid.

17. Crowley and Hegarty, p.12.

18. Kevin Kennedy, 'Heterology as Aesthetics: Bataille, Sovereign Art and the

Affirmation of Impossibility', *Theory, Culture & Society*, Vol. 35. No.4–5, pp. 115–134.

19. Noys, p.115.

20. Ibid.